A
Harlequin
Romance

OTHER
Harlequin Romances
by LUCY GILLEN

GENTLE TYRANT

by

LUCY GILLEN

HARLEQUIN BOOKS   TORONTO
WINNIPEG

Harlequin edition published November 1975

SBN 373-01928-9

Original hard cover edition published in 1973
by Mills & Boon Limited.

Printed in Canada

CHAPTER ONE

LAURIE was already half turned in the saddle before last-minute recognition pulled her up short, her back stiff and straight, and resentment in every line of her slender body. It showed too in her deep blue eyes as she held her head high, a light wind lifting the black hair from her neck and tossing it into a wild mane that fell in part over her forehead and gave her an almost primitive beauty. She fitted so perfectly into her surroundings that it was difficult to imagine her anywhere else.

The neat little bay mare she rode would have extended a more warm welcome to the newcomers, recognising her stablemate, but her rider held the reins too firmly to allow her to do so, with hands that were much too tightly clenched.

'Miss Blair!'

The voice called her again and, while she could not completely ignore it, she could and did refuse the encouragement of turning her head to greet him. She had no doubt at all of the identity of the newcomer and that it was Quin McAdam who was about to join her. She would, too, have rather it had been anyone but him, no matter if her grandfather did accuse her of being unsociable towards him. She could not bring herself to be any different.

He rode up alongside her and, sneaking a sidelong look at him from under her lashes, she was forced, however grudgingly, to recognise and acknowledge the confident ease with which he sat the big grey he rode. There was an air of arrogant self-confidence about him that even the big stallion would not dare to challenge, and it was one of the reasons for Laurie's dislike of him.

He always, somehow, managed to make her feel so small and insignificant, and as if her resentment and dislike of him were regrettable but quite understandable. Possibly even amusing at times. He was, in fact, smiling at her now, in that imperturbable, self-confident way that angered her.

His hair was so fair that it looked almost white in the bright sun, and his light grey eyes, almost ice-like in the deeply tanned face, regarded her steadily. The warmth of expression in them at the moment, she suspected, was mostly amusement at her attitude towards him, and she hastily averted her own eyes, sweeping down the long lashes to hide the expression of dislike she knew was there.

'Going my way?' he asked, and regarded her with a speculative and tolerant gaze, as he always did.

That hint of tolerance was another reason why she disliked him, had he but realised it, for it would have been so much more satisfactory for her if he had been less tolerant. If only he had not so evidently realised just how she felt about losing Clach Aros, and sympathised, she could have hated him with an easy conscience. A harsh and uncompromising lack of un-

6

derstanding would have been so much easier to deal with.

'I'm not sure which way I am going yet,' she told him, as discouragingly as possible. 'I'm just riding, Mr. McAdam, and I'm not in any particular hurry, either.'

She remembered the number of times in the past month when she had seen him riding like fury across the open moor, as if both he and his mount answered some irresistible call. Not for anything would she have him know that the sight of them flying along in the distance, so completely in harmony and looking not quite real, had filled her with a strange and disturbing sense of excitement.

'I'm not in a hurry either,' he assured her, still smiling.

His deep and, she had to admit, rather pleasant voice, was tinged with the faintest of accents, betraying a number of youthful years spent in Canada. He had confided as much to her grandfather. His easy and immediate friendship with her grandfather was another point against him, in Laurie's eyes, for she felt that her one solace in the loss of Clach Aros was not as completely in sympathy with her as he should have been.

'Is it O.K. if I tag along with you?' he asked, and she could see no reasonable way of refusing.

'I can hardly stop you if you want to come,' she told him ungraciously. 'After all, it *is* your land we're on, isn't it?'

He made no reply for a moment, but the glance he gave at her unfriendly face recognised her resentment and the reason for it. He rode beside her for a while, holding the grey to a pace better suited to her own

7

smaller mount, and she carefully kept her gaze straight ahead of her and her chin angled discouragingly.

She would have been forced to admit, had she been quite honest, that her dislike of him stemmed almost entirely from the fact that he was the new owner of Clach Aros. He was the one who had actually bought the house, and her feelings would have been precisely the same towards anyone who took away the house and lands that had been in her family for nearly three hundred years.

In any other circumstances she would probably have found him a very attractive man, despite his arrogance. But as it was he stood not the remotest chance of being even liked, as far as Laurie was concerned, although some small niggling twinge of conscience sometimes told her she was probably being unreasonable about it.

She had loved Clach Aros so much that parting with it had been heartbreaking, and she had wept bitterly when her grandfather had told her of his decision to put it on the market. He could not, he explained, maintain the old house any longer and he would not let it fall into dereliction as so many others had done.

There had been very little time to dwell on the possibility of the old man changing his mind about it, for the offer from the McAdam brothers had come almost at once. So, with a few remnants of furniture and the more necessary comforts of life, the two of them had moved into the small lodge at the far end of the tree-lined drive.

It was the last step down for the Blairs, Laurie realised bitterly. Less than fifty years before the castle had been sold to pay the heavy expenses and duties for the rest of the estate, and the family had moved into the old house. Now they were reduced to living in practically the smallest building on the estate, while this interloper and his brothers had moved in and become the proud owners of Clach Aros. Laurie saw it as the last humiliating step and resented it bitterly, although her grandfather seemed to have accepted it far more passively and appeared much less disturbed by the move.

It was also rumoured that the newcomers had also bought the castle, which was now a thriving hotel. Whatever the truth of that was, Quinton McAdam, as the estate manager of the brothers' partnership, had decided to take the house after only one viewing, and had signed the contract without delay.

It had been he too who had taken the unexpected step of allowing Laurie and her grandfather the freedom of the estate. He had also suggested that Laurie might still like to ride the little bay mare she was so fond of and could not possibly take with her. The mare could still be stabled in her old quarters, he said, and Laurie could have her whenever she wanted.

It was an invitation she would, in her resentment, have refused, but she had always had a soft spot for Brownie and she could not resist the opportunity to take her out sometimes. It was, ironically, this last generous offer that had condemned him even further in Laurie's eyes, for she saw it only as an empty and rather patronising gesture, designed to salve his conscience.

It would have been unthinkable to live anywhere

else but in the proximity of Clach Aros, and the little lodge cottage had proved less uncomfortable than she had expected, although she missed the space and graciousness of the old house. As her grandfather was seemingly content enough, she supposed she should have been too, but somehow the idea of this tall, ice-eyed stranger living in her beloved Clach Aros angered her beyond reason, and she could not hide it.

There were compensations, of course, like the view of the seemingly endless moor stretched out before them as they crested the brow of a low rise, with the soft greeny-blue swell of the distant hills sweeping upwards into the mellow summer sky, patterned with still white clouds. And the dark gleam of Cummin Loch laid like a huge mirror on the summer green turf and heather, looking only a short walk away, instead of the two miles or so it really was.

Although she had lived there all her life, the country still enchanted her with its ever-changing face. It was always beautiful, with a timeless and enduring beauty that could adapt ro anything the elements provided, from the warm-scented summer days, as now, to the bleak, cruel winters that glittered with ice and obliterated all sign of life with deep snow.

She could not, she felt sure, have lived anywhere else and been happy and content. Not that she really felt either at the moment, although the familiar panorama was already having some effect on her mood as it always did.

She was aware suddenly, as they paused at the top of the rise, that her companion was looking at her, almost tentatively, as if he was unsure whether or not to speak of something that was in his mind. And that in itself was unusual enough to make her curious.

'How are you settling down in the lodge?' he asked, and she looked at him sharply, suspecting that was not what was primarily in his mind.

'As well as we can,' she told him. 'It's not easy to adjust, but——' She shrugged, leaving the rest of the sentence unsaid.

'Your grandfather seems to have adapted very well,' he said, and there was a faint smile round his mouth, as if to suggest that she had been less adaptable. 'He tells me he quite enjoys it.'

Laurie looked at him, her blue eyes darkly shadowed. 'What else could you expect him to say?' she asked bitterly. 'He's a proud man and he's making the best of a bad job, because he knows he has to.'

'But you're determined *not* to,' Quin McAdam said softly, and smiled wryly when she glared at him.

'You have no right to make remarks like that,' she told him.

'But you *have* made up your mind not to settle down there, haven't you?' he asked.

'Clach Aros is—was my home,' she told him, her voice husky with emotion when she spoke of it. 'I loved the old house, and I hated leaving it.'

'As your grandfather, I expect.'

She looked at him warily, recognising again that he was laying the blame for her unhappiness at her own door. 'He does miss it, of course,' she said. 'But I—I don't think he feels quite so badly about it as I do.'

'Either that or he has the intelligence to accept things as they are.'

'Hobson's choice!' Laurie retorted sharply, and he smiled again.

'Possibly,' he agreed. 'But wisdom comes with age, so they say. If it's necessary to live in the lodge, your grandfather has enough wisdom to accept the fact, and make the best of it. Why won't you try and do the same, Miss Blair?'

She stared at him for several minutes, at a loss for words, when it came to trying to make him understand how she felt. 'Oh, you wouldn't understand,' she told him despairingly at last.

'I understand perfectly,' he told her quietly. 'What I can't understand is the almost psychopathic hatred you've developed for me, just because I—we bought Clach Aros. It simply isn't reasonable.'

'You wouldn't understand,' she said again, keeping her face averted.

'I know how you must feel,' he acknowledged. 'But it requires a great deal of money to keep up these old places, you must realise that.'

'I do realise it.' Her bottom lip was trembling so that she bit on it hastily before he realised how near to tears she was.

She looked like a strange and beautiful mixture of child and woman, with her black hair tossed in the wind, and the dark, shiny threat of tears in her deep blue eyes. Quin McAdam watched her for a moment with a warmth in his eyes for the wild, gamin beauty of her, then shook his head slowly.

'Your grandfather tells me you're talking of taking a job,' he said then, and Laurie turned her head and looked at him suspiciously.

'He told you that?' She hated the idea of being discussed in her absence, by this interloping stranger. 'He had no right to talk about my affairs with a perfect stranger.'

'Oh, for heaven's sake, child, stop sitting on your dignity!' Exasperation lent an edge to his voice and a harder, impatient look to his eyes, so that she hesitated to object to the way he called her 'child'. 'The fact simply happened to crop up one day in conversation, and I suggested that you might like to work for my brother.'

Laurie looked at him for a moment uncertainly, her lips parted in surprise, her eyes wide and only half believing. 'You—you thought I might——' she began, and he nodded briskly.

'Russ, my eldest brother, needs a secretary, and as your grandfather tells me you can type and do shorthand, I thought you might be interested in working at Clach Aros, that's all. Now stop bristling like an indignant hedgehog, Laurie, and consider it seriously.'

His use of her christian name, combined with his manner, gave her a confusing few minutes, and she tried to think clearly. She had no desperate need to work, it was true, but the idea of doing so was really a form of defiance for her circumstances.

She refused to merely be reduced to genteel poverty without doing something to help herself. Also, vaguely at the back of her mind, was the quite unlikely and ambitious idea of one day being able to buy back Clach Aros and living there again—although the salary of a shorthand-typist was unlikely to meet that demand.

Certainly there would be advantages to working at

the house and being so close to home at the same time. The only drawback that she could see was that she had never met either of his brothers yet, and she imagined they would be only slightly varied versions of him, and therefore not exactly the type of employer she had in mind.

'Does—does your brother know you're going to ask me?' she ventured, and he smiled, as if he already sensed her weakening.

'He knows I intend asking you when I have the chance,' he told her. 'I don't often have the opportunity of speaking to you.'

She urged the bay mare down the gentle slope, her mind tossing the idea to and fro as she tried to decide what to do. The idea of working at the house appealed to her, she had to admit, and perhaps his brother was not too much like him.

'I—I'd like to see your brother,' she said at last when he joined her, the two horses jogging along gently, side by side.

He raised one brow and smiled. 'Even if it's only to see how much like me he is?' he guessed softly, and Laurie bit her lip at being read so accurately. 'You don't like me, do you, Laurie?'

She refused to look at him, but kept her eyes resolutely on the rolling magnificence of the scenery around them, wishing he would not watch her so closely. 'You can't altogether blame me for not liking you,' she told him shortly. 'You do rather go out of your way to be as annoying as possible, don't you?'

'Do I?'

She turned then and looked at him steadily, feeling

a flick of some strange elation when she met his eyes. 'You know you do,' she challenged, and he laughed softly.

'Well, give Russ a chance,' he said. 'He's not a bit like me, I promise you.'

Laurie considered for a moment, hoping he told the truth. 'Very well, Mr. McAdam,' she said, 'I'll come and see your brother and see if he thinks I'll suit him.'

He ran his cool, expressive gaze over her from head to foot and smiled slowly. 'Oh, you'll suit him,' he said. 'But don't take my word for it. Come up about three this afternoon, will you?'

Laurie had never been interviewed for a job before, although she had learned shorthand and typing as part of her school curriculum. Miss Robertson had believed in equipping her young ladies for all eventualities, and secretarial work was very ladylike, she considered, if they should ever be brought to earning their own livings.

Laurie thought her grandfather looked at her rather anxiously as she gave a final experimental swing to her black hair before setting off along the drive to the house, and she kissed him reassuringly and smiled.

'Don't worry, Grandpa,' she told him. 'I'll probably be sent off with a flea in my ear if his brother *does* turn out to be like him. But at least Quin McAdam won't have the satisfaction of saying that I refused to try for the job.'

Her grandfather shook his head at her, but smiled as he watched her walk up the familiar gravel drive to the house, a suspicious brightness in his eyes for the proud way she carried her head, and the slim straightness of her back.

Laurie herself felt as if there was a solid, cold lump of ice in the pit of her stomach, and realised, as she got nearer the house that she really wanted this job, no matter how off-hand she had been about it to Quin McAdam.

There was a heart-aching familiarity about the big, dark oak doors, and it was hardest of all to have to ring the bell and wait for admittance instead of running up the two worn stone steps and straight into the big panelled hall.

It was only seconds before the door opened, and Quin McAdam smiled down at her, stepping back to allow her to come inside. 'He's waiting,' was all he said, but he seemed in no particular hurry.

It was over a month since Laurie had been inside Clach Aros and it seemed as if nothing had changed. There were one or two different pieces of furniture in the hall, certainly, but they had been able to take very little with them to the lodge and apparently their taste had suited the McAdam brothers well enough for them to leave it unchanged.

The same mellow dark wood smelling of wax and glowing in the dimmer light of the hall. The wide sweep of the old staircase with most of the old Blair ancestors still looking down from the walls. There was no room in the cottage for those huge oil paintings and apparently the McAdams were either bereft of painted ancestors of their own or were content to leave the Blairs in occupation for the time being.

Even the big shaggy rugs were still there, and the huge grandfather clock she had loved so much as a child. For a moment she felt a lump in her throat at the sight of it all, and when she looked at Quin McAdam she saw an understanding softness in his eyes which was quite unexpected and not a little weakening to her composure.

He said nothing, but turned after a moment or so and led the way across the hall to what had once been a small and seldom used sitting-room. It was furnished now as an office, although several of the original arm-chairs still stood against the walls, but the enormous fireplace had been panelled in and an electric fire put in the hearth.

The man at the desk did not get up when they came in, but he smiled and extended a hand when his brother introduced him. It took Laurie several minutes to realise that Russell McAdam was confined to a wheelchair, and she wondered what stroke of misfortune had put him there.

He was possibly about forty years old, and quite like his brother superficially, although much less blond and certainly less arrogant, but there were sharp lines that drew at his mouth and long deep furrows beside a rather aristocratic nose. A man who had suffered, Laurie guessed, and liked him as instinctively as she disliked the younger man.

'Please sit down, Miss Blair,' he told her. 'I'm so glad you decided to come and see me.'

'Mr.—your brother said you needed a secretary,' Laurie said. 'I hope you don't think I'm here under false colours Mr. McAdam. I mean I've been trained, at school, but I've never actually had a job before.'

He smiled reassuringly. 'Have you any idea what your speeds were?' he asked, and she nodded.

'Fifty typing, and about——' She bit her lip anxiously, trying to remember. 'I can't remember exactly what my shorthand speed was, I'm afraid, but I was top of my class and I expect I could soon pick up again.'

'Well, actually your typing is what matters most to me,' Russell McAdam assured her. 'I'm one of those strange people who would much rather write down in longhand than dictate.' A wide, pleasant smile encompassed her. 'I can't think and talk at the same time.'

Laurie smiled, encouraged. 'I don't think I could either,' she told him, and he laughed.

'Do you think you'd like to work here?' he asked then, and she knew he was thinking of how she was probably feeling, being back in familiar surroundings.

'I—I think so,' she said. 'But I think I should impress on you, Mr. McAdam, that I haven't done anything with my shorthand or typing since I left school. Will I be—fast enough for you?'

Russ McAdam smiled, his gaze sweeping over her face. 'It can't be so many years since you left school, surely,' he suggested gently. 'You're very young, my dear.'

For a moment she could have sworn she detected a faint likeness to his brother in his comment and she flushed defensively, her chin uptilted. 'I'm twenty-one,' she informed him, and almost sensed his brother smiling, even though she did not look at him.

'Well, I think you'll do fine, Miss Blair,' Russ told

her gently. 'We'll get along well enough, I think, and I'm sure you'll soon pick up speed as you go along.'

'Thank you.' Laurie was aware of Quin McAdam just behind her still, his long length leaned lazily against the door, and she wondered at his having stayed for so long.

'Aren't you going to give Miss Blair a test of some sort, Russ?' he asked his brother. 'I mean, she might be kidding you.'

Russ shook his head, vaguely displeased at the suggestion. 'That won't be necessary,' he told him. 'I'm sure Miss Blair wouldn't lie about what she can do, and I'm almost as much concerned with liking my secretary as with her other abilities. When can you start, Miss Blair?'

A little bewildered by the speed of it all, Laurie blinked for a moment uncertainly. 'Well—any time, I suppose,' she said at last. 'I'm free to start any time, Mr. McAdam.'

'Then how about starting in the morning?' he suggested. 'It would start you off with a nice short week and break you in gradually. A good idea?'

'Lovely—thank you,' Laurie said, her mind whirling. 'I'll be here in the morning. Oh—er—what time?'

'About nine o'clock?' She nodded. 'Good, then I'll see you in the morning about nine, Miss Blair.'

'Thank you.' She stood up. 'Goodbye, Mr. McAdam.'

Her new employer looked at her smilingly, leaning back in his wheelchair, his rather nice grey eyes looking at her speculatively from below their thick brows. 'Would you like to look around the old place while

19

you're here?' he asked softly. 'I'm sure Quin would willingly show you around, if you'd like to see how little we've changed it.'

'I—I could see from the hall,' she said, uncertain if she either wanted to be shown round or have Quin as her guide. 'And in here too, it's all very much the same.'

The grey eyes were kindly and understanding. 'You love Clach Aros, don't you?' he asked. 'I'm sorry—I mean I'm genuinely sorry that it was necessary for you to have to give it up, but we shall treat the old place with the respect it deserves, I can promise you that.'

Laurie felt a suspicious lump in her throat. He was so much more kind and human than his brother. 'Thank you,' she said again huskily. 'I—I know you will.'

'Would you like to walk round?' he asked, and she glanced at his brother before shaking her head slowly.

'I—I don't think so,' she said. 'Not yet—I don't think I really want to yet.'

'I understand.' He smiled at her again. 'You'll get used to being here again when you're working for us,' he added.

'Yes, yes, I expect I will.' She glanced at Quin, a hasty glance from beneath her heavy lashes. 'I expect it seems a bit silly to some people,' she said. 'But I really did hate leaving Clach Aros and—and it takes a bit of getting used to.'

'Of course it does.' He too glanced at his brother. 'Don't blame us too much, my dear. Someone had to buy it, and at least you know we shall look after it and appreciate it, don't you?'

'Yes.' She felt very small and vulnerable with Quin McAdam's tall figure towering over her, and wanted very much to go somewhere quiet and private and cry like a baby, all because Russ had been so kind and understanding.

'I'll take you home.' The offer was unexpected and she looked up hastily at the ice-grey eyes watching her, a small, quiet smile just touching his mouth.

'There's no need,' she told him, and added, 'thank you,' as an afterthought.

Nevertheless he walked with her to the door and down the steps to the drive, then she turned her head and looked at him, wondering if he meant to accompany her anyway. 'You'll be happy working for Russ,' he told her suddenly, and she smiled instinctively.

'I think I shall,' she agreed. 'I like him.'

He laughed softly, his fingertips just touching her arm as he walked beside her along the drive. 'I thought you would,' he said. 'I told you he wasn't much like me, and he isn't, is he?'

She deliberately misunderstood him, and pursed her lips in consideration. 'You look quite a lot alike,' she said.

'We were more alike to look at until Russ shattered his legs in a car crash.' He sounded suddenly harsh and bitter, as if the accident had been his own.

'I'm—I'm sorry.' She was not quite sure whether to leave the subject or pursue it.

Quin made the decision for her, however, by laughing shortly and dismissing it. 'He's better looking than me,' he declared. 'That should be a point in his favour.'

'And he's not as fair as you are,' Laurie said. 'But

21

otherwise there's a definite likeness.'

'He isn't as bossy either, you think?' he suggested, and smiled. '*That* makes a big difference, doesn't it?'

He was seemingly bent on trying to bait her into an argument and Laurie stuck out her chin. 'It certainly does,' she agreed shortly.

'In which case,' he told her with a smile, 'you should like Rod better than either of us. He's the charmer of the clan, and more your age too.'

'Rod?'

'My youngest brother,' he explained. 'The afterthought, we always called him, because he arrived more than twelve years after I did.'

'Oh, I see.' She chanced being thought inquisitive and looked up at him. 'He doesn't live here with you?'

'Not at the moment, no. He's been away for the past month tidying up loose ends, but he'll be here next week and I'm quite sure he'll approve of you being taken on. Rod's what is known as a romantic, I believe.'

'Is that bad?' She sounded vaguely on the defensive because she had always thought of herself as something of a romantic and she disliked the hint of patronage she thought she detected.

He shrugged, one brow raised, suspecting how she felt. 'It depends on your point of view, I guess. In business it can be a bit of a drawback.'

'And you don't like romantics?'

He shrugged again, a small slow smile tilting the corner of his mouth as he looked down at her. 'Again it depends,' he said.

'*You're* not one, obviously.'

'Me?' He laughed shortly. 'Not me,' he agreed. 'I

learned my business acumen in a much harder school than Rod did, and I've knocked around a damned sight more too. I've no rosy illusions about anything, even about beautiful girls. Rod automatically thinks they're helpless and need protection.'

'But not you?'

He was laughing at her, she felt sure, and she could not imagine what on earth had possessed her to become involved in such a conversation with him. 'Not me,' he said.

'He sounds rather charming and—and gallant,' she told him, her nose in the air because he was belittling something she felt was altogether desirable in a man. 'I'm looking forward to meeting him.'

'Well, you should hit it off, both being of the same mind,' he told her. 'And he's a walkover for any beautiful girl, so you'll be able to wrap him right round your little finger with no trouble at all. For one thing he's feeling much more conscience-stricken about taking over Clach Aros than Russ and I are, so you'll have that in common too.'

Laurie looked at him reproachfully from under her lashes, her eyes darkly blue. 'You shouldn't sound so—so disparaging,' she told him. 'He is your brother, after all.'

He laughed softly, and his light eyes studied her speculatively for a moment. 'Oh, don't you worry about Rod,' he told her quietly. 'He can take care of himself, romantic or not.'

CHAPTER TWO

HER grandfather was quite delighted when Laurie told him about her successful application for the post of secretary to the eldest McAdam brother. 'He's much nicer than the other one,' she told him. 'Pleasanter and more understanding. I felt really at ease with him.'

'He's crippled in some way, isn't he?' her grandfather asked, and Laurie looked at him in surprise at his knowledge.

'Yes, he is,' she agreed. 'But how did you know that?'

The old man smiled. 'Quin told me,' he informed her blandly. 'At least he told me that his brother was confined to a wheelchair. I didn't like to ask the reason.'

Laurie made a wry face as she set the table for dinner. 'You seem to be on very chatty terms with Quin McAdam,' she said, unable to keep the note of disapproval out of her voice, a fact that her grandfather noticed, looking at her with a sly smile and a hint of mischief in his faded blue eyes.

'I like him,' he told her. 'I know you don't approve, Laurie, but he's really a nice young man, and very friendly.'

'Nice,' Laurie said tartly, banging down the cruet

24

on the table, 'is *not* the word I'd use for Quin McAdam.'

'You're prejudiced,' her grandfather accused, and she shrugged.

'Maybe I am, but I don't like his manners. He's arrogant and ill-mannered.'

'He's mebbe a wee bit—rugged in his ways,' the old man conceded. 'But that'll be from all those years in Canada when he was a youngster.'

Laurie smiled wryly, shaking her head over the excuse. 'Grandpa, Canada isn't the rough, tough pioneering backwoods it was in your young days,' she informed him. 'It's an advanced, civilised country.'

'Maybe,' her grandfather allowed, 'but there's still a great deal of it that's untamed country, my dear, and Quin McAdam's seen most of it, and done most things in his time too.'

'To hear you talk you'd think he was as old as Methuselah!' Laurie remarked teasingly, amused despite her dislike of the subject under discussion, and interested too, although she would never have admitted it.

'He's thirty-four,' the old man replied promptly, and grinned wickedly at her, going on before she could question his authority. 'I asked him,' he told her.

'Grandpa! You didn't! But why, for heaven's sake?'

He shrugged carelessly, his eyes still hinting mischief. 'I was interested,' he told her. 'Good a reason as any, isn't it?'

She pulled a face, wondering how much of their own history he had imparted in return. 'So he's been telling you his life history, has he?' she said dryly, and the old man nodded.

'He's been around, that feller. Ranching, lumber-jacking, things like that, that are far more likely to give a man a rugged outlook on life than train him up in smooth, drawing-room manners.'

Laurie looked at him curiously, under no delusion that the jibe had been aimed at her for her criticism, and she pursed her mouth disapprovingly. 'I don't think good manners are to be sneered at,' she told him. 'And I'm surprised at you admiring his lack of them, Grandpa. Your own manners are impeccable, how can you make them sound undesirable?'

'I'm not saying they're undesirable,' the old man argued, with that elusive twinkle still in his eyes. 'But they're not the be-all and end-all of a man, Laurie, that's all I'm saying.'

'All right,' she conceded, 'so you admire Quin McAdam for his—his rough and ready manners.' She laughed shortly. 'You *have* been having some heart-to-hearts with him, haven't you?'

He nodded, smiling at her expression. 'We get on pretty well together,' he informed her. 'And he has been very decent to us, you know, Laurie.'

'Decent? Oh, you mean about giving us a more or less free run of the grounds.'

'And letting you keep Brownie,' he reminded her.

'Very magnanimous of him.' Laurie frowned at the reminder. 'But I don't still own Brownie, you know, and I'm more inclined to think, now that I've met his brother, that the gesture came from Russell rather than Quin—your friend.'

'My friend,' the old man echoed. 'I like to think he

is, Laurie. He's responsible for the safe keeping of my old home, and I think he'll love it in time as much as we do.'

'Huh!' Laurie's look doubted that, and she carefully arranged knives and forks on the table as if it required all her attention. It gave her a strangely lost and lonely feeling to know that her grandfather, who should have been her ally, was apparently firmly ensconced in the enemy camp.

Her grandfather sighed, his eyes watching her shrewdly as she disappeared into the tiny kitchen. 'Oh well, if you've made up your mind to dislike him, my girl, there's no use trying to convince you otherwise, is there?'

'No use at all,' Laurie declared, taking a pie from the oven and carrying it in. 'I don't like Quin McAdam, no matter how much you think of him, but I *do* like his brother Russell, and I'm rather looking forward to meeting the youngest one next week.'

'Ah yes, you haven't met him yet, have you?'

She shook her head. 'Not yet, he's away on some kind of business, so I gather, but Quin—your friend—says I'll like him best.'

'Oh, does he?' The old man looked curious. 'Why? Any special reason?'

She shrugged. 'According to his brother, he's a romantic.'

'Oh, really?' The old man's brows elevated expressively. 'Is that what he told you?'

Laurie nodded, cutting into the pie and releasing a cloud of fragrant steam. 'That's what he told me,' she agreed. 'And I should imagine they must be rather at odds if it's true, because Quin McAdam is just about as *un*romantic as it's possible to be.'

'Oh, I don't know,' the old man smiled, not looking at her as he spoke. 'I should say he'd be a very romantic kind of man if he put his mind to it.'

Laurie was surprised to find herself so nervous as she got herself ready the following morning. For one thing, of course, she had never yet had to go out and earn her own living, and she prayed that her training had not been completely lost during the three years since she left school. She could not bear the humiliation of it, she thought, if she found she was no use after all. Perhaps, in that one instance, Quin McAdam had been right—she should have had a test to see if she was good enough, before his brother engaged her.

She was uncertain, too, just how she should present herself this morning. Did she just walk in and go straight to the office, or should she ring the bell and wait to be admitted, as she had yesterday? She had no previous experience to guide her even, and her legs were shaking in the most dismaying way, as she went up the two steps to the front door.

The decision of what to do was taken from her, however, by the door being opened before she could either ring the bell or hesitate, and she looked up into Quin McAdam's ice-grey eyes. She had taken care not to dress too ostentatiously, but had thought that a navy linen dress, rather severely cut, and with a lace collar, would be most suitable, even if it did make her look rather older than her twenty-one years.

She had brushed her hair until it shone like black

silk, and then tied it back with a navy scarf in the nape of her neck. She thought, and hoped, that she looked like a very businesslike secretary and that no one would suspect just how nervous and insecure she felt.

One look at Quin McAdam's smile, however, was enough to tell her that he knew exactly how she felt and he invited her in with his gaze going over her slowly from head to toe and back, his smile broadening when he got back to her hair.

'Good morning,' he said solemnly. 'You look madly efficient.'

Laurie bit her lip determinedly. She had no wish to start off her first morning in her very first job, by quarrelling with her employer's brother, but the temptation was almost too much to resist. Instead, however, she compromised with a reply that was polite but at the same time left him in no doubt of her opinion of him.

'I hoped I did, Mr. McAdam,' she said with deceptive mildness. 'Thank you for confirming it.'

She thought for a minute that he was going to laugh out loud, but instead he merely smiled and confined the laughter to his eyes, which glittered at her wickedly. 'Let's hope you're as good as you look,' he said.

He led the way across the hall and opened the door of the office without a preliminary knock, stepping back to allow her to go in first. Russell McAdam welcomed her with a wide and encouraging smile, as he put down the telephone receiver. 'Come in, Miss Blair,' he told her. 'You're bright and early.'

Laurie responded to the smile, feeling better already, and reaffirming her liking for the older brother.

'I've always understood that punctuality was part of being a good secretary, Mr. McAdam,' she told him. 'So I thought I should start off on the right foot.'

'And quite right too,' he agreed. The friendly grey eyes regarded her for a second curiously. 'Are you nervous?' he asked, and smiled encouragement when she nodded. 'Please don't be—I shan't eat you.'

Laurie smiled warily. 'I—it's my first job ever,' she explained. 'I'm so afraid of not knowing what to do.'

'Just go along at your own pace,' he told her. 'You'll soon get the idea, I'm sure of it, and we'll get along famously.' He looked up at his brother, still standing in the doorway. 'Did you want to see me about something, Quin?' he asked.

'No.' The fair head shook slowly, while he looked from Laurie to his brother and back again. 'I just wanted to see you safely settled in with your very efficient secretary.'

Russell, Laurie thought, suspected sarcasm. For herself she was sure of it, and she looked over her shoulder at him and frowned discouragingly. 'I *hope* I'm efficient, Mr. McAdam,' she told him. 'If I'm less than perfect to start with, I'm hoping Mr. McAdam will bear with me.'

'Of course I will,' Russell assured her, and laughed. 'And I really think we shall have to get all this Mr. McAdam business sorted out before we become hopelessly confused. More so when Rod comes back today.'

'Today?' Quin pounced on the information. 'I thought he wasn't due back until tomorrow at the very earliest, next week more likely.'

'He wasn't,' Russell agreed. 'But that was him on the

30

phone just now. He says he's cleared everything up and he's coming up on the morning train. He'll be here this evening some time.'

'I see.'

Quin sounded doubtful, and Russell looked at him and shook his head. 'Rod knows what he's doing, Quin,' he told him quietly. 'You really must learn to trust him.'

Quin shrugged, a wry smile on his lips. 'Let him grow up, you mean?' he said, and laughed. 'Maybe you're right. O.K., Russ, I get the message.'

'About this name business,' Russell said, reverting to the earlier subject. 'I think in the circumstances it'd be easier all round if we used christian names, Miss Blair.'

'Laurie,' Quin said firmly, behind her, before she could suggest it herself, and grinned when she turned and frowned at him. 'Sauce for the goose,' he quoted. 'Fair enough?'

'Of course, Mr McAdam.'

The ice-grey eyes sparkled wickedly. 'Quin,' he insisted softly, and she looked at him for a moment in silence.

'Quin,' she echoed obediently.

'Well, now that's sorted out,' Russell said lightly. 'Let's get on with some work shall we, Laurie?' He looked at her curiously for a moment, as if he had just thought of something else. 'Does no one call you Laura?' he asked, and she shook her head.

'Never,' she told him. 'I was named for my grandfather, you see, and he's always been Laurie Blair—so am I.'

'I see.' He smiled. 'Ah well, it's a very pretty name and it suits you well.'

Laurie said nothing, but she thought she heard a quiet chuckle behind her as Quin closed the door after himself.

Her first day at work had gone better than she expected, even hoped, it would, and Laurie was feeling rather pleased with herself. Her shorthand had been much less rusty than she had feared and the typing skill came back to her easily. Of course Russell's patience and understanding had had a lot to do with it, and she wondered if she would have fared as well if she had been working for his brother.

It had been Russell's idea that she should take Brownie out for a while and blow the day's cobwebs away, since she was unused to spending all day indoors, and she thought this was yet another example of his understanding. She could imagine nothing better than a ride on Brownie after dinner.

She had left off work about four-thirty, much earlier than she had expected to, and in plenty of time to cook an evening meal for herself and her grandfather. After dinner she went round to the stables at the back of the house and fetched Brownie from her stall, promising that they should ride out as far as Cummin Loch and enjoy the evening breezes.

It was a lovely evening, with the sun still bright and warm, but tempered by a soft west wind that lifted her hair from her neck and gentled on her skin like a caress. The loch looked even nearer in the heavier shadows of evening and spread out like a silken patch, catching the sun as it slipped lower down in the greeny-blue sky. It was still, with the utter stillness of tranquillity, and only a slight grey frown of clouds sat on the brows of the distant hills, as if there was rain in the offing. Brownie made her way surefootedly across the familiar ground, no more impatient than her rider, but content to be out here in the quiet day's end.

A slight pressure with her heels and Laurie sent the mare forward into a faster pace, encouraging her with soft words. The mare responded and lengthened her stride gradually, making the soft turf fly in small clods from her hooves, her mane flying out in imitation of her rider's hair; heading for the mirrored expanse of the loch.

Neither of them noticed that another rider was coming up from their left, and they were almost at the loch's edge before Laurie realised they had company, frowning her dislike of the intrusion, particularly when she realised who it was. She had no special desire for anyone's company in this haven of peace and quiet, and least of all Quin McAdam's.

She dismounted and walked to the very edge of the loch, not even turning her head, hoping her silence would discourage him enough to send him away again. Not that she shouldn't have known better. The big grey looked much less mettlesome than usual, and dipped his head gratefully to drink from the loch, although his rider allowed him only a short drink before drawing him back.

A swift and surreptitious glance showed her that Quin himself looked much less jaunty than usual and rather tired, as if he had ridden long and hard in the hot sun. His shirt was opened well down too, to catch the cool of that soft west wind off the water. They had, Laurie realised, been gone all day and were probably both a lot more tired than they looked.

Quin looked at her steadily as he dismounted and allowed his horse that brief refreshment. 'Hello, Laurie.'

The greeting was so unusually subdued that she stared at him for a moment before answering. 'Hello,' she said then, and moved uneasily when, drawing the grey back from the water and over-indulgence, he stood close beside her. His unusual quietness puzzled, and she had to admit, worried her to a certain extent. 'Is—is something wrong?' she asked.

'Wrong?' The ice-grey eyes regarded her curiously. 'How do you mean—wrong?'

Laurie shrugged, more uneasy than ever when she thought she had been mistaken. 'I—I don't know,' she said. 'I just thought you seemed—worried, quiet.' She used her hands in a gesture of resignation. 'Oh, I don't know, you just seemed unusually sober for you, that's all.'

A raised brow restored the first glimmer of normality. 'Am I usually so boisterous?' he asked, obviously out of temper about something. 'You make it sound as if I usually behave either like a schoolboy or a clown.'

'I meant nothing of the sort,' she retorted, turning from him, and angry because he had not only disturbed her peace but roused that inevitable resentment in her again.

He said nothing for a moment, then he followed her

34

to where she stood kicking at the white stones that edged the water. 'I guess I am a bit off at the moment,' he admitted with surprising frankness. 'Although I didn't know it showed.'

Laurie was not to be so easily pacified, however, and she looked at the strong brown face with its incongruous grey eyes, frowning still. 'I suppose I should have minded my own business,' she said shortly.

'Maybe you should,' he allowed with a wry smile. 'But as you've noticed something amiss, I might as well tell you why I'm a bit—quiet.'

'You don't have to!'

'I know I don't,' he retorted, 'but you started it, so you can listen to the reason now. I've just had to sack a man, and it leaves a bad taste.'

She looked at him for a moment, wondering whether the bad taste was left by having to dismiss the man from his work, or from the reason for the dismissal, but it would have been unthinkable to ask which it was. 'I see,' she said instead, and saw him look at her sharply.

'You don't approve of sacking people?' he asked.

'How can I possibly approve or otherwise,' she asked, reasonably enough, she thought, 'when I don't know the circumstances?'

'Thieving,' he told her bluntly. 'From the Castle Hotel—which you know, of course.'

'Of course.'

'But you still don't approve?'

Laurie looked at him briefly, then lowered her eyes. 'I didn't say that,' she denied. 'And you know your own business best.'

'I'd better,' he said dryly. 'So why that faintly disapproving look in your eyes?'

She shrugged. 'Not because you dismissed a man for stealing,' she said. 'It was just that——' She hesitated to go on.

'Hmm?'

'I—I think you could be completely ruthless, that's all,' she told him, and meant every word of it. 'And I pity that man for that reason.'

'I see.' He sought and held her gaze. 'So, somehow or other, it's bound to come back to me being the villain of the piece, right?'

'I didn't say that either,' she denied. 'But since you mention it, I have to admit that I'm very glad I work for Russ and not for you.'

'Oh, are you?' He looked as if he was undecided whether to laugh or lose his temper and, out here on the wide solitary expanse of the moor, she hoped it wasn't the latter.

'I—I am,' she affirmed. 'Otherwise you might be sacking me.'

He laughed shortly. 'That's quite likely,' he told her. 'Have you been thieving? Already?'

'No, I have *not*!' she declared indignantly. 'And you have no right to say such a thing, Mr. McAdam.'

'Quin,' he stated firmly. 'We've been through all that, remember?'

'I remember,' she said. 'But——'

'Then use it,' he said, 'otherwise you'll get confused.'

Laurie took a very deep breath and plunged in. 'To make a distinction,' she argued, 'one needs only to give a different name to each person, and it would solve it just as well if I call your brother Russ. Then I can distinguish you, and still give *you* your full name.'

He looked at her steadily for a moment or two down the length of his arrogant nose, then he nodded slowly. 'Yes, and you would too, wouldn't you?' he said. 'You unsociable little devil!'

'How dare you?' Laurie demanded, her cheeks flushed angrily.

'Quite easily,' he told her softly. 'You go out of your way to ask for it.'

'How dare you speak to me like that?'

There was a hard, bright gleam in his eyes and his smile owed little to good humour as he surveyed her from his vastly superior height. 'You're a bad-tempered, unsociable, self-opinionated little autocrat,' he informed her with obvious satisfaction. 'And don't throw your weight about with me, Madam Hoity, or I'll take steps to bring you down a peg or two. I've had a hard day and I'm in no mood to take your little-girl tantrums. O.K.?'

'You—you——' Words failed her and she resorted to the only other means of revenge open to her. She raised her right hand and slapped it viciously hard across his face.

The ensuing stony silence she found almost fright-ening and her hands were trembling when she looked up at his face. His wide, slightly crooked mouth wore a smile that was more threat than promise, and his eyes really were icy as he looked down at her. Then he swept his gaze over her in one swift, disconcerting appraisal.

'Right,' he said quietly. 'Have it your way, lady, but

don't say I didn't warn you.' He turned and swung himself up into the saddle, then put his heels to the grey, but pausing briefly beside the browsing mare.

'No!'

It took her a second or two to realise what he had done and by the time she ran forward it was too late to do anything even if she could have. Brownie was already on her way across the moor beside her stablemate, the rein held firmly in Quin McAdam's hand.

'Enjoy your walk!' The words drifted back to her and she caught a vague, brief glimpse of a smile before he turned away and urged the two animals to greater speed.

It was only two miles from Cummin Loch, Laurie knew, or she had always thought so, but now with the whole of it stretched out before her it seemed more like five or six miles. The sun was much less hot now and she thanked heaven for that much at least, but she was still not inclined to walk so far just because Quin McAdam had seen fit to put her afoot.

She enjoyed walking usually, but she felt angry and almost tearfully humiliated as she made her way back home, vowing the most awful revenge on her tormentor. She would not even have the satisfaction of accusing him of stealing her horse, because Brownie no longer belonged to her but to the McAdams' stable.

Gradually, as was inevitable, she became less and less angry as the peace and beauty of the moor enfolded her, and she was feeling almost content when she spotted someone coming across the moor on horseback. There was no mistaking the bay mare, nor the fair head of her rider, and she set her features once more into an expression of dislike. If he had come out again just to taunt her, she would not let him get away with it so easily.

She was more than half-way home now, and having come so far she was quite happy to walk the rest, but she would not be followed and teased by Quin McAdam. She wished her grandfather could see the way he had treated her, then perhaps he would not be so ready to align himself with the enemy.

Brownie came like the wind, flat out in a full gallop, and Laurie was once again forced to recognise the perfect horsemanship of the rider. No doubt long practice in far more gruelling circumstances than this had given him such skill, but it was quite exciting to watch for all that, and she kept her eyes on him as he came towards her.

He reined in just short of her, a hint of smile on his face when she pointedly ignored him and walked on. 'Had enough?' he asked, and she looked at him meaningly from under her lashes.

'I'm quite capable of walking a couple of miles without falling down,' she informed him coolly, and veered round the two of them, with her nose in the air.

'You haven't walked two miles yet,' he told her. 'Only about half of it.'

'I can manage the rest of it,' she said, and looked up at him as he rode along beside her. 'I can't imagine why you came out again,' she told him, and he smiled.

'Can't you?' The ice grey eyes looked at her steadily and he shook his head. 'I know you won't believe this,' he said, 'but I do have a conscience.'

'I *don't* believe it,' she assured him.

39

'Well, nevertheless it's true, and I just couldn't sit down to my well-earned dinner with the thought of you wending your weary way back across the moors on foot. So I came to fetch you.'

She looked at him curiously, a frown between her brows. 'With only one horse?' she asked.

'I wasn't going to bring the grey out again,' he said. 'He'd had a hard day too, and it wasn't his fault you and I had words. So I just brought Brownie.'

'It wasn't *my* fault we had words either,' she declared. 'But you didn't bother about me, did you?'

He grinned, a disturbingly engaging grin that showed so white in the brown face. 'I bothered enough to come back and fetch you,' he told her.

'You're going to let *me* go back on Brownie and you'll walk?'

She knew perfectly well that that was not his intention at all, but the alternative did disturbing things to her senses and she told herself she would rather walk all the way than ride double with him.

He shook his head. 'Brownie can manage both of us,' he said, and put down an inviting hand. 'Come on.'

Laurie shook her head firmly, determined not to put herself in such a position. 'No, thank you,' she said. 'I'll walk the rest.'

He put the proffered hand on his hip and surveyed her from above as if he would like to do something about her stubbornness and was not quite sure what. 'So you're pig-headed as well, are you?' he commented, and Laurie glared up at him.

'If you like,' she told him haughtily. 'You've already put me afoot and treated me as if I was a—a naughty child, now I'm pigheaded as well as all the other names you called me back there. I can well do without you or your conscience, *Mr.* McAdam. Now please go away and leave me in peace.'

She glanced at him briefly again and saw that there was that icy look in his eyes again, feeling a flick of anxiety that she had aroused his temper again. 'I was right about you too,' he said quietly. 'You just won't accept an apology, will you? You have to have the last word, every time.'

'You *haven't* apologised,' she retorted, and he sighed, as if his patience was rapidly running out.

'All right,' he said slowly and with exaggerated patience. 'I'm sorry I took Brownie and I'm sorry I said some of the things I did, now will you stop bearing a grudge and let me take you home? I want my dinner.'

'Then go and have it,' Laurie told him.

'You——' She heard him take in a long, slow breath, then he bent low and a second later an arm came round her, lifting her off her feet.

'No, no! Let me go! Quin, put me down, let me go!'

He dumped her without ceremony on the saddle in front of him and put his heels to the willing Brownie, his face set in a determined hardness that for a moment startled her. 'Sit still and be quiet,' he told her shortly. 'I promised your grandfather I'd come and fetch you, and I'm going to whether you kick and scream or not.'

Since she was doing neither, she looked at him indignantly, finding the grim face rather disconcerting at such close quarters. He said nothing more and she felt very small and vulnerable with his arms round her, holding on to him with one hand, aware that she could feel the strong, steady beat of his heart under her fingers.

'I'm not kicking or screaming,' she ventured mildly, after several minutes, and hastily lowered her eyes when he looked at her.

'I had noticed,' he said wryly. 'I was breathing relief in fact.'

'Did—did Grandpa ask you to come and fetch me?' she asked, and he laughed.

'Yes, he did. I told him what I'd done and he seemed a bit startled that I'd had the nerve to tackle you, but he was a bit worried too, so I said I'd come back for you after I'd parked Hamish in his stall, and—here I am.'

'I see.'

One brow was cocked quizzically at her, and he smiled in a way that suggested all manner of things. 'Disappointed?' he asked softly, and Laurie glared at him.

'So you lied when you said you had a conscience,' she said, and he laughed again.

'Not really,' he told her. 'I *would* have come back for you whether I'd seen your grandfather or not.'

'Would you?'

The ice-grey eyes were looking at her with a strange kind of intensity and they were much too close for comfort so that she wished she could draw her own away instead of meeting them head on. 'What do you think?' he asked softly.

They were within a few dozen yards of the lodge

cottage and she wondered if her grandfather could see them from the windows, as Quin slid down and then reached up his hands for her. He held her for quite a while after she stood on the ground, his hands almost meeting round her tiny waist, then he smiled slowly and shook his head.

'You're going to be a lot of trouble to me, Laurie Blair,' he said softly, and brushed his lips gently against her mouth. 'A lot more trouble than I'd anticipated.'

CHAPTER THREE

IT was such a lovely morning the following day and Laurie was up early, musing on the idea of going for a ride before starting work. There would be plenty of time, because she did not start until nine o'clock and it would perhaps do something to banish the rather restless feeling she had this morning. Her grandfather raised a brow when she spoke of it at breakfast time, but he made no comment.

Now that she had to spend so much of the day indoors she could not ride during the day as she was used to doing, and riding always made her feel better when she was even slightly out of temper. She was reticent about seeing Quin McAdam again this morning, but that, she thought, could hardly account for the restlessness.

The gesture he had made when they parted last night could hardly be called a kiss, but it had disturbed her self-confidence more than she cared to admit and her grandfather had witnessed it with a smile she did not care to interpret, but he made no comment, and for that at least, she thanked heaven.

Later on, while she was saddling Brownie, she noticed that the grey was already missing from his stall and pursed her lips in surprise. It would seem that she was not the only one with an inclination to ride early this morning—Quin was abroad too.

The thought crossed her mind that she might meet him while she was out and she paused momentarily, then a moment later shrugged her shoulders. Even if she did meet him, which was not inevitable, it was no reason to allow herself to be deterred from her own ride.

The sun was already quite warm and promised another lovely day with not a sign of cloud in the sky. She wore no jacket nor had she anything on her head, but revelled in the mellowness of the morning as she rode, allowing the peace of her surroundings to work its magic on her as it usually did.

She took Brownie at a gentle trot out towards the loch, although she had no time to go all the way there this morning, but the mare needed little or no guidance over such familiar ground, and she could daydream to her heart's content.

She wondered briefly where Quin could have gone to so early in the day, but immediately shrugged him out of her mind. It was too nice a day to think about anyone as disrupting as Quin McAdam. They went just about half-way to the loch and then she turned the mare for home again, although she did so with reluctance when she saw the cool darkness of the water just stirring in the soft, warm wind.

As she expected it would, the ride banished most of her restlessness and she felt much more relaxed as she rode back, taking it as easily as time allowed before she was needed for the day. She was within a couple of hundred yards of Clach Aros when she saw a grey horse coming towards her from the right, and recognised Hamish, the mount Quin always rode.

She frowned curiously, for although the rider was tall in the saddle and fair-haired she was pretty sure it was not Quin McAdam, and it could not be Russ. This man rode well, but not as well as Quin, and she smiled wryly to herself for admitting that.

He seemed to increase his pace when he saw her, and came at a gallop, apparently intending to join her, so that she reined Brownie to a halt to wait for him. He was a younger version of Quin, she saw when he got nearer, and quite a lot younger, she guessed, probably not much more than her own age.

His hair was not quite so bleached fair by the sun and it grew much longer, and his eyes were a less startling light grey in the tanned face. His face too was much less tanned and weathered than Quin's, but there could be no mistaking a relationship and she knew she was looking at Rod McAdam.

Instinctively she smiled and he brought the grey right up close alongside Brownie, his gaze unashamedly interested, an appreciative gleam taking in the freshness of her complexion. and the bright, deep blue of her eyes set in dark lashes.

'Hello,' he said, returning the smile with interest.

Laurie nodded. 'Hello.' He was, she realised, much more conventionally good-looking than either of his brothers, too.

'Don't tell me,' he said. 'You're Laurie—Miss Blair.'

'I'm Laurie Blair,' she agreed, and proffered a hand which he took and held for rather longer than was necessary, his fingers curled tightly over hers.

'Rod McAdam,' he said, confirming her guess. 'You'll have been told I was coming, I expect.'

She nodded. 'Rather earlier than you were expected, I believe,' she told him, and he smiled, bobbing his head in a curiously old-fashioned manner, reminiscent of a bow.

'I'd have come much sooner if I'd realised what was in store for me here,' he vowed, with outrageous but flattering earnestness, and Laurie thought wildly that he was a young man who wasted little time with preliminaries.

She remembered, as he gazed at her with a rather dreamy expression in his eyes, that Quin had said he was a romantic, and it was not difficult to believe it, having seen him. He certainly looked the part, probably intentionally.

His long fair hair came well below the collar of a pale blue shirt that was nothing like the practical, open-necked variety his brother wore. It looked as if it was made of some soft, silky material and had long points to the collar which was turned up a little at the back. He did not wear a tie but had a silk scarf tied at his throat and flowing down over his chest. The sleeves of the shirt he wore to their full length and fastened at the cuff, not rolled up as Quin did. He was less practical and, she had to admit, much more romantic-looking, and she liked him. He was also very attractive and probably knew it.

'Do you always ride in the mornings?' he asked, and Laurie shook her head.

'Not usually as early as this,' she told him. 'But un-

47

til yesterday I could ride any time I liked during the day.' She smiled wryly. 'Now I'm a working girl I have to fit it in as I can.'

He frowned then, and looked at her with soulful eyes, so that she was reminded that Quin had also said Rod was a lot more conscience-stricken about taking over Clach Aros than either he or Russ were. 'I feel rather awful about your home,' he said. 'Please believe how sorry I am, Miss Blair.'

'Oh no, please,' Laurie begged, embarrassed as well as feeling rather tearful at being reminded. 'It—it was something that had to happen, and I know you and your brothers will—look after the old place.'

'We most certainly will,' he assured her earnestly. 'I promise you, Miss Blair.'

'Laurie,' she told him with a smile. 'Your brothers call me by my christian name because it was easier if I used theirs, to save confusion with the three of you. Quin said sauce for the goose, etc. . . .'

'Quin would,' he observed dryly, his eyes still watching her dreamily, so that she glanced at her watch hastily, rather disconcerted by his attention.

'I'd better hurry back,' she said with a laugh. 'I'd hate to be late on only my second day.'

'Oh, I shouldn't worry too much about it,' he advised blithely. 'Russ isn't a slavedriver, and you do work for *him*, don't you?' He smiled, looking at her from the corners of his eyes in conspiratorial fashion as they moved the horses off towards home again. 'Now if it was Quin you worked for,' he added, 'that would be a different story altogether.'

The remark only echoed her own sentiments, but

48

she wondered at him being quite so forthcoming on such short acquaintance. 'It probably would,' she said non-committally.

He glanced at her as they rode towards the stables, his expression curious and, she thought, a little amused. 'How do you get along with Quin?' he asked, and she wondered again what prompted the question.

'Fairly well,' she allowed cautiously, and he laughed.

'A little better than that, isn't it?' he said, and she stared at him uncomprehendingly.

'Oh?'

Rod McAdam smiled knowingly. 'I'm just going by the signs, that's all,' he told her. 'I guessed, for instance, that you would be something pretty special.'

'Did you?' It was difficult to know quite how to respond to such obvious flattery, and he laughed again.

'Well, for one thing,' he explained, 'he confirmed Russ's opinion that you were beautiful, and that in itself is rare enough to raise brows.' He turned those dreamy-looking eyes on her again. 'Now that I've met you, of course,' he added, 'I can see why.'

Laurie found the idea of Quin McAdam saying anything as personal and flattering as that about her, rather hard to believe, and she was inclined to think that this rather attractive and unsettling man must have read the signs wrongly. So she made no comment on it, but merely smiled.

When they arrived back he insisted on unsaddling Brownie for her while she went back to the lodge to change out of her riding clothes and get ready for the working day. She put on the same navy blue dress she had worn yesterday, but after a brief study of herself in the mirror, decided to leave her hair loose about her shoulders. Although she told herself it had nothing to do with the fact that Rod McAdam would almost certainly prefer it that way.

When she got to the house this time there was no sign of Quin to let her in, but she rang the bell and an elderly housekeeper admitted her. Laurie thought the woman looked vaguely concerned about something and it took her only a couple of seconds to realise what it was.

Angry voices were being raised behind the office door. Or more accurately, one angry voice and one defensive one. She had no difficulty in recognising Quin's as the angry one, and she guessed the one on the defensive would be Rod, evidently having fallen foul of his brother's temper.

The quiet soothing voice that joined the group a second later she recognised as undoubtedly belonging to Russ, but what on earth could be causing such a fracas at this time in the morning she could not even guess. She had not, until now, visualised the brothers quarrelling among themselves, although when she thought about it she supposed there were bound to be occasional outbursts.

While she still hesitated she heard Quin's voice again, harsh with anger, so that she could all too easily imagine how icy hard his eyes looked, and shivered in sympathy with his youngest brother. 'Just don't take Hamish again without asking me first,' Quin told him, evidently far from pacified, despite Russ's efforts.

Laurie, an unwilling listener, realised then that it was because Rod had taken the horse he always rode when he was working, and she was forced to admit that his objection was reasonable enough in the circumstances. Although she still felt sorry for Rod for having incurred his wrath.

'Couldn't you have taken Brownie for this morning?' she heard Russ ask, his quieter voice only just audible through the thick wooden door, and she bit her lip when she realised that she too had inadvertently contributed to the quarrel.

'I could have if Laurie hadn't taken her,' he retorted.

'Oh, I see.'

'Not that I'm blaming Laurie,' Quin added, unexpectedly charitable. 'She couldn't have known I'd want the mare this morning because Rod hadn't any more sense than to take out the one and only horse to go traipsing around on.'

'I wasn't traipsing around,' Rod defended himself, and Laurie almost jumped out of her skin when the housekeeper's voice spoke beside her.

'Ye can find ye're own way in, can ye not?' she asked.

Laurie looked at her doubtfully. 'Do—do you think I should?' she asked, and the woman nodded, smiling at her.

'Oh aye,' she told her. 'It'll be all right.'

Laurie glanced at the office door again, her eyes uncertain. 'I don't know,' she demurred. 'I don't like to interrupt.'

The woman shook her head and smiled again, sounding very sure of her facts. 'Oh, it's no as bad as it sounds, Miss Blair, don't ye worry.'

'But I—I don't think I should just—go in,' Laurie

said, not at all anxious to be caught up in the seemingly violent emotions on the other side of the door. 'I mean, shouldn't I wait until someone comes out?'

'Don't let the hot words worry ye,' the woman told her. 'They soon get over it, and all the sooner for someone going in there.'

'But——' Laurie still hesitated, unwilling to be the one who broke in on a family quarrel, especially as Quin was involved.

'They'll be as right as rain in a couple of hours,' the housekeeper assured her with a smile. 'An' not a sulk between them, either. That's the truth, ma dear.'

Laurie looked at her curiously, intrigued by her certainty. 'You seem very sure about that,' she said. 'You sound as if you know them very well.'

The housekeeper nodded. 'That I do,' she told her. 'I've been with the McAdam family ever since Mr. Russ was a laddie. I know these outbursts, they never last very long, and your going in there will stop them all the sooner. Ye take ma word for it, Miss Blair.'

Laurie smiled warily. 'If you think so,' she said. 'But I feel a bit like Daniel going into the lions' den.'

The woman's homely face beamed encouragement at her, and Laurie walked across to the office door and raised a hand to knock. A very brief and telling silence followed her knock, then someone spoke.

'Come in!'

The order was brief and peremptory, and she guessed it came from Quin. When she opened the door, after taking a very deep breath, three pairs of grey eyes turned on her at once and she only just resisted a temptation to turn and run out again. Russ smiled at her, however, apparently the least disturbed of the three and she went right into the room.

'Come in, Laurie,' he told her, and flicked a barely perceptible glance of warning at his brothers. 'I'm afraid we haven't noticed the time. What's more, I'm ashamed to confess that I'd even forgotten you were coming.'

'Oh well, I can——' she began, but Russ waved a hand and shook his head.

'No, no, my dear, please stay.'

She hesitated for only a second longer, then walked over to her own desk and put down her handbag, very much aware of Quin's icy gaze as she did so. 'I hope I'm not too early,' she ventured, looking at Russ, as the most likely one to encourage her. 'I mean if I've interrupted anything im——'

'Nothing important,' Russ assured her, and glanced at his youngest brother with a smile, determined to restore normality. 'I understand you've met Rod already,' he said, and Laurie nodded, responding to Rod's smile.

'Yes, I have,' she said. 'We were both out riding early this morning.'

'Taking the only two available horses,' Quin said tartly, before anyone else could speak, and she looked at him and blinked, wondering if, despite his earlier defence of her action, he was going to quarrel with her too.

'I'm sorry,' she told him, sounding much more meek than in fact she felt. 'But I didn't realise Rod had taken the grey, not until it was too late.'

'Would it have made any difference if you had?'

53

She felt the colour grow in her cheeks as she fought with a rising temper. 'I expect it would,' she said shortly. 'But I didn't realise you'd need Brownie.'

'I needed a horse,' he informed her shortly. 'I could have made do with Brownie, if she'd been there.'

'Well, I'm sorry,' Laurie told him. 'But as you said —you can't really blame me.'

He cocked a curious brow at her and his mouth crooked in to a dry smile. 'So you heard *that*, did you?'

Laurie glared at him. 'I couldn't *help* hearing, the way you were shouting,' she retorted. 'I'm sorry you were left without a mount, but it won't happen again, I promise you. I won't ride either of your horses again without your express permission, Mr. McAdam.'

For a moment he said nothing, only looked at her, though with rather less surprise than his brothers did, then he laughed. 'O.K., O.K.,' he said. 'You don't have to make the big sacrifice, Laurie. And for heaven's sake, don't look so long-suffering.'

'I wasn't intending to *be* long-suffering,' Laurie informed him. 'But Rod has more right to take out one of the horses than I have, and I'll just make sure that you're never left without one in future, that's all. After all, they *are* yours now, not mine.'

'Oh, for God's sake, you little idiot!' The light eyes showed signs of returning anger. 'Stop acting the martyr, Laurie, I don't want the mare. She wouldn't be much good to me, anyway, because she hasn't enough stamina to take me around all day, as Hamish does. Whether Rod wants her for his early morning jaunts is something you'll work out between you— I've got work to do.'

Russ sighed, with relief Laurie guessed, and leaned back in his chair. 'Yes, we all have,' he said. 'Can you get on with something, Laurie, while I have a word with Rod for a few minutes?'

Laurie nodded, sitting down at her desk and pointedly ignoring Quin's speculative gaze fixed on her. Rod moved over to discuss some matter with Russ and, after a brief hesitation, Quin came over and stood in front of her desk, looking down at her, a faint smile on his face, willing her to look up.

'Laurie.'

She did not look up, but carefully sandwiched carbon and paper together and wound them into the typewriter, her voice cool and distant when she spoke. 'Yes, Mr. McAdam?'

A large hand clamped down on the roller and prevented her from doing anything else, and she looked up at last, reluctantly. He was leaning over her desk, a glitter in his eyes that challenged her to object, a small tight smile round his mouth still. 'I don't like being ignored when I'm carrying the flag of truce,' he told her, soft-voiced. 'And if you call me Mr. McAdam like that just once more I shall deal with your pigheaded discrimination in no uncertain way. Understood?'

'Pigheaded discrimination?' she echoed, and he nodded.

'If you called Russ, Mr. McAdam too, in deference to his years,' he said, 'I'd forgive you, and I can understand you being informal with Rod because you're much of the same age and he's very obviously smitten with you, as I expected he would be. But if you can give *both* of them the friendly treatment and not me, the man in the middle, then I object.'

'You——' Laurie began, but he raised a commanding hand, and silenced her.

'I don't see why you should have your knife in me,' he went on relentlessly, 'to the extent that you use that cool, toffee-nosed *Mr.* McAdam, as if I was something the tide washed in.'

For a moment she said nothing, then she met his eyes and, for some inexplicable reason, felt like laughing. It bubbled up inside her and showed in her eyes, bright and unmistakable, and Quin leaned further over the desk and put a hand under her chin.

'So,' he said softly. 'You find that idea appeals to your sense of humour, do you?' His fingers gripped her chin hard and she hastily lowered her eyes to hide the betraying laughter.

'The idea that you're something the tide washed in?' she asked. 'Yes, I do rather, *Mr.* McAdam.'

'Why, you little——' He laughed suddenly and withdrew his hold abruptly, straightening up and running his fingers through his hair, as if he was suddenly aware that there were other people in the room. 'One day,' he vowed, *sotto voce*, 'I'll know what you're all about, Laurie Blair—in the meantime I've got work to do.'

'So have I.'

He grinned down at her. 'Take it easy on Rod, won't you?' he said, still too quietly for his brother to hear what he said. 'He's very susceptible.'

'He's very attractive.'

She wasn't quite sure what made her say that, but

he held her gaze for a moment longer, then smiled wryly and nodded his head. 'Yes, I thought you'd think so,' he told her, and turned and walked out of the room without a backward glance.

By the time Laurie had been working for Russ McAdam for two weeks, she was quite accustomed to the different routine it entailed, and found she enjoyed it far more than she had expected to. Her employer was always polite and considerate and she found that Rod McAdam was even more charming on closer acquaintance.

He had ensured that neither of them had to do without their rides or incurred Quin's anger again, by buying a beautiful black Arab horse. It was a stroke of extravagance that Laurie was to learn was typical of Rod, if not of his brothers. Several times they had ridden together, both before and after working hours, although Brownie was poor competition for the newcomer when it came to speed.

Rod appeared to divide his working time between his two brothers, more or less equally, although she knew he preferred to be with Russ. Partly, so he told her, because when he was in the office with Russ he was also with Laurie, but his preference was also influenced, she suspected, by the fact that Russ had a great deal more patience with him than Quin had.

It was with some surprise that she found Rod waiting in the hall for her one morning when she arrived, and looking rather more serious than usual, although he smiled when he saw her. 'Good morning, Laurie.' He took her hand and looked down into her eyes in the way he always did, but there was an air of something different about him and she looked at him curiously.

'Is there something wrong?' she asked, and he shrugged.

'Not exactly wrong,' he told her, leading her back to the front door with a hand under her arm. 'Just a bit strained. We have an unexpected visitor and I don't think Russ'll be wanting you this morning. Not yet awhile anyway.' He took her back out of the house and down the steps to the gravel driveway where he stopped and took both her hands in his. 'Why don't you go and change,' he suggested, 'and we'll go for a ride while we have the opportunity?'

Laurie looked at him doubtfully, although the idea appealed to her immensely. 'But will it be all right?' she asked. 'I mean, shouldn't I be here in case Russ wants me for anything?'

Rod shook his head. 'Better not,' he told her, and Laurie frowned.

'It all sounds very mysterious,' she told him. 'Have you got a V.I.P. staying here that I mustn't see?'

'Not quite that,' Rod smiled. 'But I should give the house a wide berth for the moment—I'm going to.'

'Oh, I see.' She was curious, but it would hardly be polite to probe any further, although she thought he realised it from her manner.

'You go and change,' he told her. 'And I'll see you here in about twenty minutes. O.K.?'

'O.K.,' she agreed.

Her grandfather looked at her in surprise when she returned, and her brief explanation for the reason intrigued him too, and he pursed his lips thoughtfully.

'It's odd,' he said. 'But maybe it's something to do with that woman I saw arriving last night.'

'A woman?' Laurie paused on her way upstairs, her interest quickened.

The old man nodded. 'I only had a glimpse of her from the window as she drove past,' he said. 'But it looked like a woman and a child. I suppose it's some family business that Rod doesn't want to mention.'

'Maybe,' Laurie agreed thoughtfully, wondering who on earth the woman could be, and which one of the two elder brothers she was there to see. Obviously it was not Rod she had come to see, for he was, as he put it, giving the house a wide berth, so it must be either Russ or Quin, or perhaps both of them. Anyway, she shrugged her shoulders, it did not concern her which one of them it was.

It was rather sooner than the appointed time when Laurie arrived back at Clach Aros and there was no sign of Rod yet, but as she approached the house the front door opened and Quin came down the steps. He was dressed as he always was, in riding breeches and an open-necked shirt with the sleeves rolled up above the elbows of his strong brown arms, and since he was leaving the house, the visitor was evidently not his.

He looked at her for a moment with cool, curious eyes, then walked down the last few yards of the drive-way to meet her, smiling in a way that made her feel horribly self-conscious. She looked slim and cool in cream trousers and a light blue cotton shirt, but she had never felt so self-conscious about the way she was dressed as she did now with those light, expressive eyes watching her.

'I see you've given yourself a day off,' he said, without preliminary greeting, and Laurie blinked indignantly at the suggestion.

'No, I haven't,' she argued. 'Rod said I wouldn't be needed this morning. It wasn't my idea at all.'

'I see, so you're riding instead.' Before she could explain further he smiled at her. 'Well, keep me company as far as Glen Cummin, will you?'

'Well——' She hesitated, wondering if Rod would be blamed for encouraging her to take advantage. 'I—I promised to meet Rod here,' she explained, and he elevated a brow into the thick fair hair on his forehead.

'Oh, I see, he's slacking too, is he?'

'We're neither of us slacking,' Laurie denied indignantly. 'I can quite easily go and change again if I'm wanted.' She half turned and would have walked off back to the lodge, but a hand on her arm restrained her.

'Whoa! Don't be in such a hurry to grab the wrong end of the stick. *You're* not wanted.' He qualified that with a smile. 'At least not for secretarial duties, but Rod is supposed to be coming with me this morning.'

'Oh, I see.'

The ice-grey eyes watched her musingly, his hand still on her arm as if he was afraid she might walk away again. 'Of course I can see his point in preferring to go riding with you,' he told her.

'I—I didn't encourage him.' She had no idea why she should have been so insistent about that, but he smiled knowingly.

'Maybe not,' he said. 'Although you'd do it without realising it, wouldn't you? You know you only have to roll those big blue eyes at Rod and he goes weak at the knees.'

'Oh, that's ridiculous!' She glared at him uneasily. 'If Rod was supposed to be coming with you he must have—have forgotten or something.'

'Or something,' he echoed dryly. 'Rod's a moral coward. He'd sooner keep out of the way when family upheavals like Rose appear on the scene.'

She had no idea who Rose was, but assumed it was the woman her grandfather had seen arriving. 'I—I guessed something was wrong,' she said, her curiosity aroused again, and Quin laughed shortly.

'You could put it like that.'

They stood on the drive, several yards from the house, but from the corner of her eye Laurie saw the front door open again and wondered if it was Rod, ready at last. She turned her head, but had time only for a brief glimpse of a tall, slim woman with brown hair before Quin reached out suddenly and pulled her into his arms.

The move was so unexpected that she did not even protest when his mouth covered hers with a hard relentlessness that set her pulses racing wildly as she was crushed against him. She heard two sounds as one, indistinctly, what seemed like hours later. One was Rod's voice sounding more surprised than indignant, and the other was the front door banging shut, and when she at last managed to free herself she closed her eyes for a moment on the dizzying sensation in her brain.

Rod was beside her when she opened her eyes again, but the woman who had appeared so briefly in the doorway had disappeared, presumably behind that angrily slammed door.

'What's the idea?' Rod asked, mildly annoyed, and Quin did not answer him for a moment, but stood looking down at Laurie, those ice-grey eyes far from cold-looking.

'Isn't there a song?' he asked lightly, at last. 'Girls are made to love and kiss, and who am I to interfere with this?' He laughed softly, a sound that trickled along Laurie's spine like an icy finger. 'You shouldn't keep a beautiful girl waiting, Rod. I was trying to lure her into coming with me instead.'

'Hard luck,' Rod told him. 'She's coming with me.'

Quin looked at him meaningly, one brow raised. 'And *you*,' he reminded him, 'were supposed to be coming with me over to Killie Sloc—or had you forgotten?'

She might just as well, Laurie thought dizzily, not be there at all, and she stuck out her chin determinedly, her deep blue eyes sparkling. 'If you're supposed to be working, Rod,' she told him, 'please go. I'd rather you didn't neglect your work for me, and I don't mind riding alone.'

'Well, I do mind you riding alone this morning,' Rod said, his eyes on his brother. 'Oh, look, Quin, it isn't that important that I come with you this morning, is it?'

Quin glanced at Laurie, then shrugged carelessly. 'It makes no difference to me,' he told Rod. 'If you're more interested in your girl-friend than in your job, that's up to you.'

Laurie would have objected to his choice of noun,

62

but before she could do so Rod protested, though not about the same thing. '*You* hadn't exactly got work on your mind when I came out of the house just now,' he pointed out. 'And it was *my* girl you were kissing too, so don't be sarcastic, Quin.'

'*Your* girl?' Now that Rod had used the term he seemed bent on doubting it.

Laurie too would have liked to make her opinion known on that point, but it seemed she was to be given little or no chance to say anything at all, between the two of them. '*My* girl,' Rod insisted, and Quin looked at Laurie with a small, slow smile that did nothing to placate her.

'True, Laurie?' he asked softly, and she lowered her eyes uneasily.

'As far as I'm concerned I don't belong to anybody,' she informed him. 'And I strongly object to both of you treating me as if I've been purchased with the rest of the property!'

'Laurie!'

It was Rod, of course, who protested so reproachfully, and she instinctively looked up at him and smiled. 'I'm sorry, Rod, but I don't like being talked about as if I was either not here or was some—some inanimate object.'

'I'm sorry.' He took her hands in his and she made no effort to free them, although Quin was watching her with that slow meaningful smile still on his face.

'Oh,' she shrugged, 'I suppose it wasn't meant like that. Maybe I'm too sensitive about it.'

'You are,' Quin assured her, before Rod could reply, and his brother glared at him darkly.

'I wish you'd stay out of this,' he told him. 'I'm going for a ride with Laurie, so there's no point in you waiting for me.'

'I see.'

He said nothing in protest about the way he was more or less being dismissed, but Laurie could see he did not altogether like it and there was a hint of ice in those tell-tale eyes again.

'Rod, if you're supposed to be working,' she began, and glanced at Quin, that small crooked smile tilting one corner of his mouth and making her feel uneasy still.

Rod too glanced at his brother, but with a look of defiance, it seemed to Laurie. 'I don't have to,' he told her. 'And I'd much rather ride with you.'

'Then I'll leave you to it,' Quin said, before she could reply. '*Some* of us have work to do.'

She felt that he was making the jibe for her benefit as much as Rod's and she shook her head hastily. 'I'd rather not go if you're supposed to be working, Rod, really.'

Surprisingly it was Quin who answered her, the cool, ice-grey eyes holding hers for a moment, and he smiled. 'Oh, don't stay on my account,' he told her. 'You go for your ride, I can manage to struggle along without Rod.' He raised a hand in a careless salute and turned to walk off. 'Be good,' he admonished softly.

Laurie watched him stride off round to the stables, her eyes uncertain, then Rod put an arm round her shoulders and they followed at a more leisurely pace. She was still curious about the strange woman in the doorway, and most of all about Quin's hasty and disconcerting reaction to her appearance.

'Penny for them.' Rod's voice close to her ear startled her out of her reverie, and she smiled as she shook her head.

'I'm afraid it's just plain, common or garden curiosity,' she confessed, and Rod tilted an eyebrow at her in an expression oddly reminiscent of Quin. 'I—I can't think why Quin'—she shrugged—'behaved the way he did just now.'

Rod made a wry face and laughed. 'That was a bit out of character, I admit,' he said. 'He usually shows a bit more finesse than that, but the reason was obvious enough.'

'Not to me,' Laurie told him. 'Unless that—that woman had something to do with it. The one I caught sight of just before—before he grabbed me.'

Rod laughed shortly. 'Oh, she was the reason,' he told her. 'He did it for the sheer hell of showing Rose what he thought of her. She was livid!'

The slamming door had been evidence of that, Laurie thought, but was still puzzled as to just who the woman was. 'Rose?' she asked, and Rod looked at her from the corners of his eyes, as if he speculated on her reaction.

'Rose,' he said, 'is Russ's ex.'

'Oh, I see.'

It was a surprise, she had to admit, although there was no earthly reason why all of them shouldn't be married, and probably were for all she knew. Russ particularly was in his late thirties, and Quin was thirty-four, so he had informed her grandfather in a burst of confidence, so it was quite probable they were married even if Rod wasn't.

Rod's fingers squeezed her arm gently. 'Puzzled?' he asked, and she nodded. 'She's ostensibly here to bring Colin, their son, to see Russ, but——' He spread his hands and lifted his shoulders, leaving the rest of the sentence unsaid.

'You mean she hopes for a reconciliation?' Laurie asked, but could not imagine, in that case, why Quin's kissing someone else had made Rose McAdam lose her temper as she had.

Rod laughed again. A short, humourless laugh that sounded most unlike him. 'Not a reconciliation with Russ,' he told her. 'It's Quin she's after, as always, and she'll manage it too one of these days, I wouldn't be surprised.'

'Oh, I see.'

Laurie said no more, but she felt a cold sensation when she thought of what could happen if she should ever have the misfortune to meet Rose McAdam. That kiss of Quin's must have given her heaven knew what ideas about them.

CHAPTER FOUR

IT was a dull, threatening sort of day and Laurie was beginning to wonder if she was wise to have come quite so far when those dark grey, heavy-looking clouds sat so gloweringly on the hills. But the threat of thunder made her feel restless, and as it was Saturday and she was free all day, she had decided to go for a ride and try to rid herself of the feeling.

Brownie seemed to sense the atmosphere of threat in the air too, and her ears were pricked for the first distant rumblings of thunder, her sensitive nose quivering as she picked her way daintily across the soft springy turf towards the loch, her hooves clicking flintily on the half-hidden stones. The water in the loch itself too, had a more leaden grey look, and appeared deeper and somehow more ominous.

Chiding herself for being fanciful, Laurie urged the mare on to a faster pace, anxious to create a more cooling breeze, and Brownie responded willingly enough. They galloped on as far as the loch and there Laurie dismounted to give her mount a moment to rest, trailing the reins and walking along the edge of the water.

She began idly tossing pebbles on to the still surface, shattering the placid mirror of it into a thousand ripples, her mind straying in a dozen different directions at once. Ever since the other morning when she had caught that brief glimpse of Rose McAdam, she had found the question of Russ's wife intriguing. She had seen nothing of her since and did not even know if she was still at Clach Aros or not, although she knew Colin, her son, was because she had seen him and spoken to him.

Rod apparently disliked his sister-in-law intensely and avoided her whenever he could, although he got on well with his nephew and indeed had introduced him to Laurie. The boy was about twelve years old and very much like his father and his two uncles, but much more shy and introverted than any of them, probably due to his mother's nature.

What Quin's feelings were in the matter, she had no idea and would not dare to venture a guess, for Quin was quite the most unpredictable of the three brothers. He had said nothing about his ex-sister-in-law to Laurie, and her grandfather had been annoyingly non-committal when she asked him if he had heard anything.

So deep in her thoughts was she that she was aware of nothing until Brownie whinnied softly and drew her attention, then she brought herself hastily back to earth and turned her head curiously. There was another rider coming in their direction, someone riding Rod's beautiful black Arab, but it wasn't Rod, she knew, because he was away for the whole day.

Also, she could see now, the rider was unmistakably a woman, and it took no great effort on her part to identify her as Rose McAdam. There was a haughty tilt to her head, with its light brown hair cut short and a blue scarf tied round it. She wore conventional riding garb of breeches and boots with a rather masculine-looking cream shirt, although there was nothing unfeminine about her. She was tall and well proportioned and the word that came instantly into Laurie's mind was formidable.

When she got to the spot where Laurie had left Brownie she reined in the Arab and looked across at Laurie, silent for a few seconds while her shrewd blue eyes studied her and made up her mind about her. Then she walked the Arab across the few intervening yards and reined him in again, looking down at Laurie with no hint of a smile.

'Good morning.' Laurie was determined to make an attempt at friendliness, no matter if she had very little encouragement.

The greeting was not returned, nor did she smile, but looked down her nose at her with those shrewd, hard eyes. 'You're the secretary, aren't you?' she asked, her opinion of the lower orders plain in her voice.

Laurie was very tempted to make some acid retort, but she did not really want to start off on the wrong foot with the woman, even if Quin had done his best to ensure just that. 'I work for Mr. Russ McAdam,' she told her quietly, admiring her own restraint.

'I'm Mrs. McAdam,' she was informed, with the obvious expectation that she would be impressed.

Laurie was uncertain whether or not to admit to knowing her identity, but she thought it was probably better if she did not. 'I'm Laurie Blair,' she said quietly instead. 'How do you do, Mrs. McAdam?'

Again there was no response to the friendly over-tures, but the hard eyes glanced at Brownie, waiting patiently. 'Is that your own animal?' she asked, and Laurie nodded, then hastily amended it.

'No, not now,' she admitted. 'She belongs to—to the McAdams.' She was unsure which of the brothers should be attributed with ownership.

'I see. Do they know you've taken it?'

Laurie flushed. 'Oh yes, of course they do! At least they know I do take her out. They allow me to ride whenever I like.'

Elegant brows expressed surprise at such democ-racy. 'Really?' A faint sneer curled the long upper lip and she swept her with a hostile look that made Laurie's blood rise angrily. 'They would,' she said.

'They understand, and they've been very kind to me,' Laurie told her, realising with a start that for the first time she was really appreciating the fact.

'No doubt that's why you take advantage of it,' Rose McAdam snapped.

'Take advantage of it?'

'I was referring to your behaviour the other morn-ing, with Mr. Quinton McAdam.'

Laurie's never very docile nature was rebelling more every minute, and she wished she could find some really crushing reply for this determinedly unfriendly woman. Her deep blue eyes glowed with anger and it showed too in her pink cheeks as she looked up at her. It was a definite disadvantage being on foot, she realised, since it automatically gave the other woman a psychological advantage.

'It was more Quin's behaviour than mine, Mrs.

McAdam,' she told her, deliberately using the abbreviation of his name. 'I was as much surprised as you were.'

'Indeed?'

'Yes, indeed,' Laurie retorted. 'I can hardly be held responsible if Quin suddenly takes it into his head to kiss me.' She realised as she said it that she actually enjoyed making the jibe, and she saw Rose McAdam's gauntly good-looking face flush angrily.

'That's a lie!' she declared vehemently.

'It's the truth,' Laurie argued, heaping on the coals. 'He simply grabbed me and kissed me without warning.'

'I don't believe you,' Rose McAdam said, her eyes blazing, and hard as stone. 'Quin wouldn't have kissed you without some encouragement.'

'Well, he did,' Laurie insisted, unconsciously provocative as she stuck her chin in the air, and dared the other woman to argue further.

Rose McAdam took a deep breath and for a second Laurie wondered what she would do. It was obvious that Quin, and anything to do with him, was an explosive subject as far as she was concerned, and she looked in danger of losing control of her temper. After a few moments, however, she seemed to realise what was happening and she regained control of her emotions. A small, tight smile showed at the corners of her mouth and she looked down her nose again at Laurie, quite plainly aware that she was much more impressive up there on horseback than Laurie could hope to be on foot.

'I'd advise you to be very careful,' she said, in a

voice dangerously soft. 'You're getting out of your depth. I believe Rod finds you attractive at the moment, doesn't he?'

Laurie nodded vaguely, uncertain where this was leading. 'I believe so,' she agreed, 'but I don't see——'

Rose McAdam narrowed her eyes. 'Then be satisfied with that, *Miss* Blair,' she told her, 'and stay out of Quin's way, or you may find you've bitten off very much more than you can chew.'

'You have no right to speak to me like that,' Laurie protested angrily. 'No right at all!'

'I have every right,' Rose McAdam insisted. 'And every reason too, since your protestations speak for themselves.'

'You have no reason either,' Laurie denied. 'I see Quin in the course of my work, as I do Russ—no more.'

'No *more*!' her antagonist sneered. 'When I catch him kissing you?'

'You didn't catch us,' Laurie retorted swiftly. 'You were already there in the doorway when Quin kissed me, and it didn't seem to worry him that you were!'

The gaunt, fine-boned face flushed again, and there was an almost fanatical light in her eyes as she held on to the reins so tightly that her knuckles showed white. Any moment now, Laurie thought wildly, she's going to lash out at me, and she felt a moment of chilling panic in the pit of her stomach at the thought of it.

'You slut!' The words were spat at her venomously and Laurie was left speechless by the malice aimed at her, as she stood there wondering if she could just walk away and take Brownie, without having to hear any more insults. Before she could act, however, Rose McAdam was speaking again, that thin, malicious smile in evidence. 'I think it's time someone put you firmly in your place, Miss Secretary,' she said. 'That mare you're riding belongs to my husband, you said.' Laurie stared at her, unable to believe that such a thing could happen to her twice within a couple of weeks. 'I'll take her back with me,' her tormentor went on, confirming her suspicions. 'You can walk.'

'No!' Laurie objected, made more angry by the knowledge that since she no longer owned Brownie she had little ground for argument, but the rain was coming nearer every minute and it was unlikely that there would be any second thoughts or qualms of conscience this time as there had been when Quin had put her afoot a couple of weeks ago.

Rose McAdam looked across at the gathering clouds, the first thunder already rumbling ominously down into the valley, as if she followed her thoughts. 'It's going to rain before very long,' she said with malicious satisfaction.

'Then you can't leave me here with no means of getting home,' Laurie protested, in vain she knew.

'I most certainly can,' she was informed. 'You have a pair of feet, you can walk back, and if you get caught in the rain—well, perhaps a good soaking will bring you down to your right size.'

'But you can't!' Laurie insisted, and started hastily across towards Brownie with the intention of mounting before the other woman could do anything about it. It was unlikely, she thought, that she would be prepared to go to the extent of dragging her bodily from Brownie's back, once she was there. But a swift pressure of heels sent the Arab across the same distance in a fraction of the time and Rose McAdam had the reins in her hand before she could get there.

Laurie watched helplessly when she rode off with both horses, calling back over her shoulder as she went. 'Maybe this will make more impression on you than just warning you to stay where you belong,' she called. 'Walk back, and I hope you get soaked to the skin!'

Laurie had gone no more than half a mile when the storm broke in earnest and in no time at all she was facing the worst downpour she ever remembered. The thunder rolled and cracked overhead, and the rain came down so hard that she could see almost nothing in front of her.

There was no shelter of any sort on the open moor where she was caught and the soft turf grew increasingly waterlogged, making it even harder going as her booted feet squelched and sank in the soft ground.

It was only after she was thoroughly wet through that she reached less open ground and the sanctuary of some trees, although it was far from ideal shelter in the circumstances with lightning crackling ominously above the tall firs.

Rose McAdam's wish that she should be soaked to the skin had certainly been granted, she thought ruefully, and shivered as she tried to pull the collar of her dripping wet shirt closer round her neck. The shirt clung to her like a second skin, and her trousers too were so wet through that they looked several shades darker than their original cream colour.

Her hair clung wetly to her head and dripped down her back as she tossed it back impatiently from her face. It was debatable which emotion was most responsible for her feeling so horribly tearful—anger or the sheer misery of feeling so wet and uncomfortable.

Crouched there in the shelter of the tall trees, she hugged herself tightly and wished that both Rose McAdam and her brother-in-law were feeling half as uncomfortable, vowing vengeance on them both at the earliest opportunity.

It was almost startlingly unexpected, therefore, when only a few minutes later she recognised the rider that came galloping through the downpour on Quin's familiar grey. He was headed for the loch and she realised a moment later, when she could see better, that he was also leading Brownie.

'Quin!'

She stepped out of the shelter of the trees and called to him, wondering if her cry had been heard above the sound and fury of the storm until she saw him turn his head, and breathed a sigh of relief. Both the grey and Brownie were urged across to where she stood just at the edge of the trees.

Quin looked almost as wet as she did herself. His fair hair looked much darker than usual and it clung tightly to his head as her own did, making a shower of glistening drops when he tossed it back impatiently from his forehead.

He was wearing a short waterproof jacket and looked even bigger than usual in its bulk, his tanned face streaming with water and looking somehow primitive in its darkness.

Both the horses were dripping wet and breathed steamily, as if they had come the whole way from Clach Aros at a full gallop, as they probably had. He slid from the saddle as he reached her and held both animals with one hand, while the other reached out to take one of hers, holding it so tightly that her fingers were crushed and the warmth of him tingled through her. Then he drew her back further under the trees, out of the worst of the rain, looking down at her steadily for a moment before he spoke.

'Are you all right?' he asked then, and she nodded.

'Yes—yes, thank you.'

Her teeth were chattering and she felt she had been put into a bath of cold water, but it was amazing how much better she felt now that she had someone else with her. He reached under his own bulky waterproof jacket and pulled out another one, smiling as he opened it out.

'I grabbed this from the stable on my way out,' he told her as he held it for her to put on. 'It isn't likely to fit you, but at least it's warmer than nothing.'

Laurie shrugged into it thankfully, uncaring that the sleeves came almost down to her elbows, or that it smelled rather of horses and liniment. It felt wonderfully warm and dry, even on top of the wet shirt. 'Ooh, that's lovely,' she told him gratefully. 'Thank you.'

He put a hand on her wet head and frowned. 'You're soaked,' he said. 'You'll be lucky if you don't get pneumonia.' He hugged her up close to his side, his arm almost completely encircling her. 'We'll *both* be lucky if we don't get pneumonia,' he added.

'Maybe that was the idea, at least as far as I'm concerned,' Laurie said shortly, and he cocked a brow at her.

'What's that supposed to imply?' he demanded, and she wondered just how much criticism he would hear against Rose McAdam.

'It implies that I was deliberately left to walk back in this storm,' she told him.

'You think so, do you?' he asked, and Laurie nodded firmly.

'I *know* so.'

She felt horribly tearful again, and realised now that it was self-pity that made her feel like crying, although she was still furiously angry when she thought of the way Rose McAdam had deliberately left her without a horse when she knew quite well what would happen to her.

After a brief frown Quin grinned at her, and there was something oddly reassuring about that grin, although it angered her. 'So you caught the rough edge of Rose's temper, did you?' he asked. 'She's quite formidable, isn't she?'

That was exactly the word Laurie had thought of, but she glared at him reproachfully. Her lashes were thick and wet from her soaking and they fringed her darkly blue eyes that glistened with anger for his taking it so lightly. With her hair limp and hanging round her face in curly tails, she had a childishly appealing look that even her anger did not dispel, and there was a strange kind of wild beauty about her.

'I don't think it's funny,' she told him reprovingly. 'I was meant to get soaked through like this. Mrs. McAdam said she hoped I would before she went off with Brownie. It was supposed to cut me down to size, so she said.'

'Oh, I see.'

'I've no doubt you do,' Laurie retorted. 'It was your fault in the first place.'

'*My* fault?' He looked at her unbelievingly. 'How *my* fault?'

'Oh, you know it was,' Laurie told him crossly. 'You waited until you saw Mrs. McAdam standing in the doorway the other morning, then you—you kissed me.'

The ice-grey eyes glowed wickedly at her, then he smiled again, slowly. 'You think so, do you?'

'Oh, stop saying that!' Laurie said, seeing any hope of getting the upper hand rapidly slipping away. It seemed quite idiotic to be standing here under the trees with his arm round her, quarrelling with him but at the same time very glad of the warm nearness of him to keep the shivering chills at bay. 'I want to go home,' she said plaintively. 'I'm soaked through to the skin and wretchedly miserable.'

'Oh, you're that all right,' he told her, looking down at her with a grin.

'Well, so would you be,' she complained, 'if you were in my state!'

'I *am* in your state, you little misery,' he told her. 'Now for heaven's sake stop complaining and be grateful for small mercies. You haven't even said a nice thank-you yet, you ungrateful little wretch. I shall be wishing I'd left you to your own devices soon.'

'It might have been better if you had in the circumstances,' Laurie told him mournfully. 'Your coming for me won't endear me any more to your—your——'

'Ex-sister-in-law?' he suggested softly.

Laurie stuck out her chin, her eyes suggesting other possibilities. 'Whatever she is,' she said, and he still smiled, although there was a warning glint in his gaze.

'My ex-sister-in-law,' he insisted. 'No matter what other tale Rod may have dreamed up and passed on to you. Right?'

'Right,' she agreed. 'Now can we *please* go?'

'I should think so,' he told her. 'But the horses needed a short breather before we started back. I pushed them a bit coming out here.'

She pulled the collar of the jacket up round her ears and hunched her shoulders into it, shivering again. 'Of course,' she said. 'Give them a few minutes longer. I'm all right.'

'You're sure?' She nodded and his arm pulled her even closer, so that she felt a little less cold.

They neither of them said anything for several seconds, then Quin caught her eye and smiled, and she hastily lowered her own gaze because something oddly disturbing was happening to her pulse and she felt suddently rather excited and lightheaded. 'We'd better get you home,' he told her then. 'I don't want you laid low with pneumonia, especially when it's my fault in the first place.'

Laurie had quite forgotten her earlier accusation and she looked at him curiously. 'Your fault?'

He grinned. 'So you said—don't you remember?

You said all this happened because I kissed you when Rose was watching.'

She remembered then and looked at him reproachfully. 'You don't have to be sarcastic about it,' she told him. 'That *was* why you did it—Rod said so.'

He flicked one brow up into the wet thatch over his forehead. 'Oh, I see,' he said. 'And Rod's word is gospel, is it?'

'Not necessarily,' she denied. 'I'd already come to the same conclusion myself.'

'You had?' He laughed softly, his arm tightening momentarily round her shoulders. 'Now if you'd asked me, I'd have said that you were too tizzied at the time to decide anything.'

'Well, I wasn't,' Laurie denied hotly. 'It was all too obvious that you just kissed me because you wanted your sister-in-law to see it.'

He said nothing for a moment, then he released his hold on the horses and turned to face her, one hand sliding round her, under that loose jacket, pulling her to him, with a small, tight smile on his face and his eyes glittering wickedly. 'Rose isn't watching now,' he said softly, and sought her mouth with his own, forcing her head back against the fingers of his other hand, his hold tightening until she felt she could not breathe.

'Quin!' She gazed at him for a moment breathlessly, her eyes wide and uncertain, then she pushed at him with both hands. 'Oh, you——!'

He was laughing, and she felt like nothing so much as hitting him, mostly, she admitted, because she felt small and vulnerable, and she had been affected by his action much more than he had apparently. 'I'll take that as payment in kind for **fetching you**,' he told her. 'Since you haven't said thank **you yet**.'

'Quin——'

He laughed again, softly, as **if at some** private joke and turned back to the horses, **bringing** Brownie round in front of the Arab. Then **he put his** hands round Laurie's waist again and lifted **her off** the ground in to the saddle.

'Up you go,' he said, not waiting to hear what she had to say. 'Then it's bed and a hot drink for you, my child, before you develop something diabolical.'

She took the reins from him and glared, sitting stiff and upright and resenting that 'my child' bitterly. The rain had eased as they rode out from under the trees, although it was still coming down quite heavily and the horses flattened their ears against it.

Laurie refused even to look at him as they moved off, the chill of her wet clothes even more uncomfortable without the warmth of Quin's arm round her to counteract the coldness. 'Put your heels to her,' he instructed, slapping Brownie sharply with his hand. 'The sooner you're home and dry the better.'

'I couldn't agree more,' Laurie said shortly, and sent the mare into a gallop, bending low against the beating rain that was still bad enough to make visibility very poor.

It was an ignominious ending to her ride, being rescued by Quin. Coming home soaking wet and humiliated by Rose McAdam's malicious jealousy, when he had been the cause of it in the first place. If he had taken it the least bit seriously it would not have been so bad, but his obvious amusement at the idea of there being any reason for Rose McAdam to be jealous of her made her feel very small indeed. Heaven knew what her grandfather would make of the incident, especially when he knew its cause.

CHAPTER FIVE

RATHER surprisingly it was Rod who made the most fuss when Laurie told him next day about her being stranded in the storm, and his dislike of Rose McAdam was even more obvious. 'She's a bitch!' he declared vehemently, his arm round Laurie's shoulders consolingly. 'She's an absolute bitch, and I only wish I'd been here yesterday. I'm terribly sorry about it, Laurie, I really am.'

'It wasn't your fault.' She pulled a face and smiled. 'I have to admit that I agree with you, though. Perhaps I shouldn't say it when she's your sister-in-law, but there's no doubt of it.'

'My *ex*-sister-in-law,' he told her. 'Thank heaven Russ had enough sense to divorce her!'

'But she still comes to stay here; doesn't Russ mind her coming?'

Rod shrugged. 'What can he do? She has custody of Colin and he likes to see him.'

'It seems a shame that Colin can't come on his own and see his father,' Laurie said. 'He's old enough to travel on his own, isn't he?'

'I suppose so,' Rod admitted, and smiled maliciously. 'But then Madame wouldn't get to see Quin, would she? And that's the prime object of the exercise, not Colin at all. As I said, she's an absolute bitch, but we put up with her for a few weeks every so often because of Colin. I'm only sorry that she's got her knife into you, though.'

'It isn't as if she has any reason for it, either,' Laurie said, and he pulled a face.

'Oh, I don't know. You're a lovely-looking girl, that's enough for her, and if she *thinks* you've got designs on Quin she'll fight you tooth and nail. Then of course Quin himself goes out of his way to be damned awkward and make things worse.'

'He does?' She was curious about how Quin treated his difficult relative.

'I'm thinking about that kiss the other morning,' Rod reminded her. 'He did that deliberately to annoy Rose, and then yesterday he gave her a piece of his mind for stranding you in that storm. Mind you,' he added, while Laurie digested that piece of information with interest, 'it isn't the same for him. Now if *I'd* been here and told her off she'd have known she'd been told off. He doesn't see things in the same way I do, of course, and anyway, he takes things in his stride more.'

'Mmm, he didn't seem unduly bothered about me being deliberately left to get soaked,' Laurie said, 'although he *did* come out for me and I never did thank him for coming.' She remembered that Quin had claimed the kiss had been payment in kind for his services, but it might be as well not to mention that part of it.

'He was in the stables when Rose came back with Brownie apparently,' Rod went on, bringing her back to earth. 'And as soon as he saw Brownie he thought something had happened to you. When Rose said what she'd done, he gave her his opinion while he saddled Hamish, then took Brownie and tore off after you.'

Laurie supposed she should have been flattered by the attention she had commanded, and she was certainly puzzled as to how Rod knew so much about what had happened, when he had not even been there. 'Who told you what happened?' she asked, and he grinned.

'McKinnon, the manager of the hotel. He was here to see something about some extra staff, and he was in the stable to find Quin when Rose came in.'

'I see.' Quin's hasty departure so soon afterwards would have done nothing to endear her to Rose McAdam, Laurie felt sure, and she wondered too what Robert McKinnon would have made of it, for she had known him since she was a child.

'He was quite staggered, apparently,' Rod told her with a grin, 'when Quin took off like that, and Rose was furious.' He laughed shortly. 'McKinnon is no more fond of Rose than I am. She's staying there, at the castle, and I gather she isn't the most popular guest they've ever had.'

Laurie gazed at him for a moment, puzzled. 'Oh, I see. She isn't staying at Clach Aros?' Somehow that made her feel better.

'Oh lord, no!' Rod declared, apparently horrified at the very idea. 'It'd be much too nerve-racking for all of us if she was. We have Colin here, but Rose is staying at the castle, although she comes here all too often unfortunately. She likes to ride, so we more or less have to offer her the use of our horses.'

'Oh, I see.'

Rod sighed. 'Oh, let's forget about Rose and her bitchiness, shall we? There must be more congenial subjects to talk about.'

Rod was sitting with her on the low wall that surrounded the garden at the back of Clach Aros. It was a fine day again after the storm, and the sun was warm and inviting, slanting through the trees and making shifting, flickering patterns across their faces as they sat there. It was a day she could have enjoyed a thousand times more if she had been the hostess and not the visitor. She would never, she told herself, get used to being a visitor at Clach Aros.

Rod, as if he guessed something of her thoughts, caught her eye and smiled. 'Is this one of your favourite perches?' he asked, and she nodded, responding to the smile, despite her nostalgia. Somehow it was not easy to mind Rod being there and she had never resented him as she had Quin. Perhaps because Quin had made the actual purchase and she could not rid herself of the idea that he had been responsible for her losing her home.

'It always was my favourite perch,' she told him. 'I used to climb the trees when I was a little girl, and I've been spanked many times for tearing my clothes on them.'

'Did you get spanked?' He reached for one of her hands and looked down at the small, fine-boned fingers. 'I can't imagine you doing anything as tomboyish as climbing trees and getting spanked for it.'

'Nevertheless I did,' she assured him with a smile. 'I believe I was quite a handful in my young days.'

Rod put an arm round her waist and hugged her, his

grey eyes glowing warmly as he looked at her. 'And now you're quite an armful,' he told her softly. 'I never really believed that girls as beautiful as you existed outside fairy stories, you know.'

Laurie smiled, uncertain how much his rather extravagant compliments suited her. He was certainly very attractive, but she was rather wary of taking him too seriously. 'Beautiful girls don't exist outside fairy tales,' she told him, and he shook his head.

'Oh, but they do,' he insisted. 'You're beautiful—even Quin admits it, and he's not given to unsolicited praise.'

'I don't believe it,' Laurie retorted swiftly, wishing that Quin need not have been brought into the conversation again. He had the most disturbing effect, even in his absence, and the idea of his thinking her beautiful did the most ridiculous things to her pulse rate. 'I'm sure he's far too blasé, or too busy, even to know what I look like.'

'Well, *I* notice what you look like,' Rod told her, prepared to dismiss Quin for more personal points. 'You're very lovely, Laurie. Much too lovely to have a boy's name.'

'It isn't a boy's name,' she denied laughingly, but he was dreamy-eyed again, his mind busy with an alternative.

'Lorelei,' he said at last, and smiled at her, well pleased with his version of her name. 'I shall call you Lorelei, it's much more appropriate for a siren as dangerously beautiful as you are.'

'I don't know that I like being called after the beauties who lure sailors to their deaths,' Laurie declared, pulling a face and laughing.

'Don't you like it?'

'Not particularly,' she said, and smiled to take the sting out of the rejection. 'I don't think I'm dangerous enough for a name like that.'

He gazed at her with his dreamy grey eyes. 'You're dangerous to me, Laurie. Dangerous to my state of mind—I've been dreaming about you ever since the first day I saw you.'

'A little over two weeks ago,' Laurie reminded him, and immediately felt rather unkind when he looked so hurt.

'Time has nothing to do with it,' he told her. 'Haven't you ever heard of love at first sight?'

'I have,' she said, 'but I don't believe in it.'

'Why not?' He looked hurt again. 'It happens, Laurie.'

'It might do occasionally,' Laurie allowed. 'But I don't think it did in your case, Rod. Not really and seriously.'

'I'm perfectly serious,' he assured her. 'I'm about to fall in love with you, beautiful Laura, whether you like it or not.'

Laurie was unsure just how she did feel about it. It would not be too difficult, she thought, to fall in love with Rod. He was good-looking and very attractive and he made her feel that she was important to him. It gave her a rather enjoyable feeling of being somebody again, after so much humiliation and disappointment lately.

'You're very good for my ego, Rod,' she told him, trying not to treat it all too seriously, and he turned her round on the wall to face him, his hands on her arms, his eyes solemn.

'I'm not trying to be good for your ego, Laurie,' he told her gravely. 'I'm falling in love with you, and I wish you'd take me seriously.'

'I—I'm sorry.' She found it difficult to know just what to say in the circumstances.

'That I'm falling in love with you?' he asked. 'I hope you're not sorry about that.'

Laurie looked at him for a moment. At the tanned face, so much more conventionally good-looking than either of his brothers, and those dreamy grey eyes that were very definitely a big part of his appeal. He had the same deep, pleasant voice they all had too, and altogether there was little she could find to fault in him. It was simply that, at the moment, she did not feel inclined to take him too seriously.

'I'm flattered if you really are falling in love with me,' she told him. 'I really am, Rod, but in a way I wish you hadn't told me. After only two weeks I can't honestly say how I feel about you, except that I like you a lot, and I like being with you.'

He gazed at her for a moment longer, then sighed deeply. 'Oh well,' he said resignedly, 'that's better than nothing, I suppose. I don't expect miracles, but if you don't actually hate me, then for the moment I'll settle for that.'

She shook her head, smiling at his solemnity. 'Oh, of course I don't hate you! I don't *hate* anybody.'

He looked at her for a moment steadily. 'Except maybe Rose?' he suggested softly, and pulled her towards him and kissed her.

It was a long, slow and quite ardent kiss, and it set

89

her pulses racing wildly, but that did not really surprise her, for she had hardly supposed she was the first girl he had kissed. Even so she had not expected to find him quite so smoothly practised, and it made her feel a little wary of him and very unsure of herself.

When he released her at last, he looked down at her for a moment, then put a hand under her chin and lifted her face to him again, smiling but a little puzzled by her response, she thought. 'You should be kissed more often,' he told her softly, and Laurie shook her head uncertainly.

'Rod, someone might see us out here.'

'So?' He flicked a querying brow that was startlingly reminiscent of Quin. 'Kiss me again, and never mind what anybody thinks or says.'

He kissed her again, this time even more passionately, so that she felt quite breathless and a little light-headed. But all the time he was kissing her she was not so much worrying about whether anyone would see them, as remembering the way Quin had kissed her, out there in the pouring rain under the trees. And it disturbed her to realise that *his* kiss had driven everything else completely from her mind.

Laurie gazed at her grandfather in dismay, her eyes wide and unbelieving. There was a heavy cold sensation in the pit of her stomach and for several minutes her brain refused to accept the fact of what he had just told her.

'I—I can't believe it,' she said, sitting down heavily in an armchair. 'They wouldn't—they *couldn't*, could they, Grandpa?'

The old man shrugged, resigned, it seemed, to the latest turn of events as he had been to all the other changes in his life during the past couple of months. 'They're entitled to do exactly as they like with the house now it's theirs,' he reminded her. 'There's nothing you can do about it, Laurie.'

'But it's—it's monstrous!' Laurie declared. 'And they *promised*, they promised they'd look after Clach Aros—love it as we did.'

Her grandfather smiled at her patiently, shaking his head. In sympathy with her feelings but realising the harder facts of reality too. 'Unfortunately, my dear,' he told her gently, 'loving a place doesn't pay for repairs and upkeep. It's hard cash that does that.'

'But they have plenty of money,' Laurie objected, feeling close to tears. 'They don't *need* to do it. A stately home!' She spoke the hackneyed title bitterly. 'How could they?'

'Necessity?' her grandfather suggested quietly. 'And it's no good upsetting yourself over it, Laurie. No use at all, my dear.'

'I *am* upset,' Laurie insisted, her blue eyes dark with anger and hurt at the thought of her beloved Clach Aros being invaded by hordes of visitors. 'And I can guess who's behind this—this money-grubbing scheme too.'

'Oh?' Her grandfather looked at her curiously, and she nodded, in no doubt at all that she was right.

'Quin,' she stated firmly. 'It has all the earmarks of his—his arrogance and insensitivity.'

'Laurie, you're——'

'I'm not wrong,' Laurie interrupted him bitterly,

91

getting to her feet. 'I know you'll stand up for him, Grandpa, but I *know* him. Just because he comes here and talks to you—tries to make friends with you, he——' She shook her head, her hands clenched tightly. 'Oh, I'm going out before I explode!'

She already felt sorry for venting her anger and disappointment on her grandfather before she had gone more than a couple of hundred yards from the cottage, but she resisted the temptation to go back and apologise, because she knew he would understand how she felt.

A walk in the cool evening air would do her good after being indoors all day too. It would help to clear her head, although she did not anticipate being any less bitter about the proposed plans to open Clach Aros to public viewing.

She had no hesitation in allotting the blame for the idea to Quin McAdam, for she could not easily imagine Rod's dreamy romanticism giving rise to anything so sordidly commercial. Russ too was unlikely to have thought of it, for he was always kindly and sensitive and she could not see him being prepared to open his home to paying customers. It just had to be Quin, with his arrogance and impatient sufferance of sentimentality, who had conceived the idea and would probably bulldoze his brothers into going along with him by sheer force of will.

She was not really surprised to find that she was crying as she walked along, although she felt convinced that her tears were as much due to anger as to sorrow, and an anger directed specifically at Quin McAdam. Lately she had found him more than usually annoying, although possibly only because she was more than normally sensitive.

Somehow it seemed to her that he smiled in a certain way whenever he saw her with his younger brother, although admittedly he had made no comment so far, but Laurie thought she sensed a certain sly amusement at the sight of them together, and she resented it bitterly.

There were several things lately that made life less placid than she would have liked it, not least the fact that Rose McAdam was still staying on at the castle and also spending a great deal of time riding with Quin when he went about his usual routine.

She made no secret of the fact that she would be far more pleased if her ex-husband's secretary was less young and presentable, and once or twice Laurie had clashed with her verbally, although so far there had been no more spiteful retaliations, as when Laurie had been stranded during the storm.

When she was not working, a great deal of Laurie's time was spent with Rod, and she grew daily more certain that eventually she would fall in love with him. He did not press too hard for her to make up her mind to be more serious about him, but he was gently persistent in his pursuit of her, and she found his attentive charm having more and more of an effect on her own emotions. She resented bitterly Quin's apparent amusement at the idea, and the fact that he always made her feel gauche and uneasy whenever he saw them together.

It annoyed her too to find that even now it was Quin who was uppermost in her mind as she walked over the moor in the direction of the loch, and not Rod. No matter if the business association with the brothers was supposed to be a partnership, Quin was the dominant factor in it, and he would not, she feared, have too much difficulty in bending the other two to his will if he put his mind to it. If Quin had made up his mind that Clach Aros was to be opened to the public, she had no doubt that the other two would eventually agree to it, whatever their own private feelings were.

She had already walked as far as the thick belt of trees between the cottage and the loch before she ralised how far she had come, and she sighed, supposing she should turn and go back. It was such a beautiful evening that she felt she should have been giving more attention to her surroundings and less to unhappy things.

The tall, dark pines were arrayed like a cluster of black shadows against the green and gold evening sky, and as much of the loch as she could see beyond them caught the westering sun and gleamed like molten gold spilled over the open moor, dappled with little winking flashes of light where the surface was ruffled by a breeze. It was much too beautiful to waste on being unhappy, and at least she could still enjoy such evenings as this and not be shut away in a town somewhere.

She walked through the edge of the trees, swinging a long, heavy stave of wood that she had picked up, deciding that she would go just as far as to where the wood curved outwards and widened, then turn and go back. Her walking made little sound beyond a soft, slightly crackly swish, and she could hear the thousand and one noises that the more permanent residents made.

Also, she realised suddenly, there was something else. Something familiar, and yet she could not, at the moment, recognise it. A restless, shifting sound as of something larger than the rabbits and birds that rustled and whistled among the lower growing vegetation.

It was an impatient, whistling snort a few seconds later that gave her the necessary clue and she realised that somewhere among the trees there was a horse getting impatient. It sounded as if it was standing, shifting impatiently from one foot to another, and the thought of someone else being in among the trees, near enough to be audible and yet making no attempt to call out a greeting, gave her an oddly creepy feeling suddenly, and she gripped the stick she carried a little more firmly as she walked on.

It took her only a second to identify Rod's black Arab horse a moment later, and she looked startled to see that he was riderless. He stood between two trees, his fine head on its arched neck tossing impatiently, his nostrils quivering warily when he saw Laurie.

She approached him warily, for he was not as docile as Brownie was and he would permit no liberties, even from Rod. 'Suli!' She spoke his name softly as she approached and extended a hand to rub his sleek black neck. 'Good boy, Suli.'

The Arab permitted her to smooth his neck, even tossed his head in appreciation, but Laurie was concerned about his being riderless, especially now that she noticed that the reins lay across his saddle and were not trailing as they would have been if his rider had merely dismounted and left him for a moment. He was restless too, although that was not too surprising, but combined with the absence of a rider it gave Laurie a cold, shivery feeling along her spine.

'Why are you here alone?' she whispered softly to the Arab, who pricked his sensitive ears. 'Who was——' She stopped then and bit on her lower lip hard, her eyes catching sight of something just behind him in the high green fronds of bracken.

She made herself take time to lift the reins over his head and draped them over a low branch, then she walked round behind him and stared down at Rose McAdam, lying still and inert on a bed of crushed bracken. A large, ugly bruise was already colouring darkly on her forehead and she looked so horribly still that Laurie was almost afraid to touch her for fear of what she might discover.

A brief and inexpert examination, however, discovered a slow but steady pulse and a reassuring rise and fall under the thin shirt, but it was essential to get help as quickly as possible, and she wished she had taken time to change and bring Brownie out instead of walking. However, there was nothing for it but to cast modesty aside and ride back on the Arab, no matter how unsuitably dressed she was.

She straightened up, shock still making her slow to act, and stared down at Rose McAdam, unable to completely believe she could have been thrown, for she had shown herself to be an excellent horsewoman whenever Laurie had seen her riding. She shook her head, to clear it, then half turned towards the waiting Arab, only to stop short when she heard someone else coming.

The drumming sound of hooves on the turf was unmistakable and she heaved a sigh of relief. Whether it was Rod or Quin, either of them would be welcome, for they could take the responsibility of the injured woman off her unwilling hands, and she looked up, her relief plain in her eyes.

It was neither of the brothers, however, and she stared rather blankly at the slight boyish figure of Colin McAdam, mounted on Brownie and almost on top of her as he came through the trees. He reined the mare in sharply and it was the fallen rider that he spotted first, not the riderless horse, his eyes widening in horror as he stared down at the still figure.

'Mother!' His voice cracked and rose shrilly, then he looked at Laurie with a glint of panic in his eyes. 'You've killed her,' he accused. 'You've killed my mother!'

'No! Oh no, Colin!' She went towards him intent on reassuring him, and realised that she was still carrying the thick stave of wood she had picked up during her walk.

The boy looked at her in alarm when she came nearer. 'You've killed her!' he whispered hoarsely.

'No, Colin! She isn't dead, she's only hurt, knocked out.' She was more concerned at the moment with reassuring him about his mother than with defending herself, but the boy seemed unable to grasp anything beyond the fact that his mother lay still and hurt on the ground and that Laurie stood over her with what must have looked like a pretty formidable weapon in her hand.

'You hit her!' He would not be convinced, and Laurie despaired of getting his help.

'Listen, Colin.' She grasped Brownie's rein, despite Colin's effort to break away. 'Your mother needs help quickly. Now ride back to the house and tell one of your uncles. Get them to call an ambulance or the doctor as quickly as possible. Do you understand?'

'I won't leave her with you,' Colin declared flatly. 'I won't let you hurt her again.'

'Colin, please!'

'No!' He got down and came and knelt beside his mother, and Laurie choked back tears at the helpless look of despair on the young face.

'Then I'll have to go,' she told him, but he took no notice of her. He did not even turn his head to protest when she took Brownie in preference to the swifter Suli. She had enough to contend with, she felt, without having to cope with possible temperament from the high-strung Arab.

It was both inelegant and uncomfortable riding in the brief summer dress she wore, but since there was nothing else for it she managed as best she could and rode like the wind back towards Clach Aros. Perhaps she should not have left a boy as young and vulnerable as Colin with an injured woman, but there was nothing else she could have done in the circumstances, and no time to argue with him.

She saw Quin before she gained the entrance and waved a hand to stop him from going into the house as he obviously meant to. Instead he came down towards her, his eyes startled when he saw her dress. Without a word he lifted her down from the saddle as soon as she stopped, and stood her on the gravel drive in front of him.

'What's wrong?' he asked briefly, and she looked at him for a split second, wondering suddenly who he would believe when it came to allotting the blame for the accident.

'It's Rose—Mrs. McAdam,' she told him. 'She's had a fall and she's unconscious in the trees over there.'

'A fall?'

Laurie nodded, a little impatiently. 'From Suli. She needs a doctor, Quin, and quickly, I think—she's had a nasty knock on the head.'

'I'll ring Doctor Sandford,' he said briefly, and turned to go into the house, leaving her there with the mare, wondering why she felt so suddenly cold and scared.

When she came round Rose McAdam would tell them that her son was mistaken in his version of what had happened. She would know that her fall had been an accident and that Laurie had had nothing to do with it, but just the same that niggling little worry persisted as she took Brownie round to the stables at the back of the house.

CHAPTER SIX

IT was a little later than usual when Laurie went up to the house the following morning, and she was hurrying along the driveway, rather out of breath, when she saw Quin coming down the front steps, obviously on his way to the stables. It would be polite, she supposed, if she asked him how Mrs. McAdam was this morning.

He stopped when he saw her, as if he guessed her intention, and waited for her to join him. She thought there seemed an unfamiliar hardness in his expression and it made her heart jolt erratically when she remembered Colin McAdam's wild accusations against her when he saw her with his mother. Quin did not smile either, even when she ventured a small, tentative one of her own, but merely looked at her speculatively, as if something was puzzling him.

'Good morning,' she said, already feeling uneasy, although she told herself she had absolutely no reason to.

'Good morning.' No more than that, she noticed, just the bare bones of politeness.

'I'm—I'm afraid I'm a bit later than usual,' she offered, wondering why she should bother to apologise to him, when it was Russ she worked for.

'Are you? I'm sure no one will notice.'

She hesitated briefly, then took the plunge. 'How's Mrs. McAdam this morning?' she asked.

The ice-grey eyes studied her for a moment longer. 'How do you think she is?' he asked quietly, and Laurie swallowed hard. He seemed bent on being difficult this morning and she looked at him curiously. A cold feeling of panic niggled at the back of her mind when she remembered Rose McAdam's still figure on the bed of bracken under the trees, and the black bruise on her forehead.

'Well—I don't know,' she said. 'I—I expect she's not feeling very good this morning after that nasty fall she had.'

'Did you actually see her fall?'

It was just too much, Laurie thought wildly. He sounded almost as if he was interrogating her, and what was more, as if he had every right to do so. 'No,' she said sharply. 'I didn't actually *see* her fall. She was lying on the ground when I found her and a fall seemed the only feasible explanation. Unless she became—I don't know, dizzy, perhaps.'

'She didn't become dizzy,' he told her quietly. 'And she says she didn't fall either.'

Laurie stared at him. He was behaving exactly as if it was a firmly established fact that she had been responsible for Rose McAdam's injuries, and surely that was ridiculous, for by now the woman herself would have given them a true picture.

'I don't understand,' she told him, warily on her dignity.

His mouth, she thought, tightened a fraction and it was the first time she ever remembered seeing him look doubtful about anything. 'There appears to be some doubt as to whether she really did fall from her horse,' he said, and Laurie eyed him warily.

She flushed a moment later when she realised what he was implying and her eyes sparkled with anger. 'Of course she did,' she said. 'I've already told you, she must have done.'

'Colin says you were holding a stick of some sort.'

'I was,' she agreed. 'I picked it up while I was walking, but as for doing anything else with it——' She looked at him for a moment, her eyes unhappy and uncertain. 'I know Colin was shocked at first,' she said. 'And he made some silly, childish accusations, but surely Mrs. McAdam herself has put that straight by now.'

Quin held her gaze steadily. 'I don't know whether she has or not,' he told her quietly. 'That's where the problem lies, you see.'

Laurie stared at him, her heart beating a wild and terrifying tattoo at her side. That small niggling doubt was showing definite signs of becoming a reality. 'But surely——' she began.

'She claims that what Colin says is true,' he went on quietly relentless. 'She says you lost your temper and attacked her with that heavy stick you were holding when Colin found you.'

'Oh no!'

'She says you hit her on the head with it and knocked her out,' he went on, 'and when she came round, Colin was with her and you were nowhere to be seen.'

'Well, of course I wasn't,' Laurie cried despairingly.

'I came to tell you—to get a doctor for her. You know that, Quin.'

'You didn't hit her?'

'No, of course not!' She stared at him, her heart racing in panic. 'Do—do you really believe I'm capable of it?' she asked, and her voice was husky—not a bit like hers at all.

He put a hand under her chin and lifted her face to him, the ice-grey eyes scanning her features narrowly. 'I find it hard to believe,' he told her. 'And yet you *are* a little firebrand, as I know to my cost, and you have taken the rough edge of Rose's tongue once or twice lately.'

'Oh! Oh, you—you——' It was infuriating not to be able to find the words she sought so urgently, and the way the tears were gathering in her eyes too was bound to give quite the wrong impression.

'Remorse or injured innocence?' he asked softly, tracing one fat rolling tear down her cheek with a gentle finger.

She knocked away his hand from her chin, rubbing vigorously at the marks it had left. 'Anyone who could turn Clach Aros into a peepshow,' she told him bitterly, 'is capable of believing anything.' She thought he looked surprised at that, but it was difficult to see anything through her tears. 'And since I'm apparently a suspicious character as far as your family's concerned,' she added, 'I'd better go back home and keep out of their way.'

'Laurie!'

She ignored him, refusing to stay and listen to him any more. If he believed her responsible for Rose

McAdam's accident, then it was possible that his brothers were of the same mind, and she was not prepared to stay and find out. She turned and walked back down the drive, her back stiff and resentful while the tears rolled unchecked down her face. She had never felt so utterly miserable and ill-used in her life, and she felt rather self-righteous about it too.

'Laurie, come back here!'

Let him shout, Laurie thought, and walked on. But when she heard him on the gravel driveway, coming after her, she increased her pace and ran. It was inevitable, of course, that he would soon gain on her with his much longer legs, and she instinctively veered off into the trees that bordered the drive, with the idea of eluding him.

It was a vain attempt, as she might have known it would be, and after only a few seconds he caught up with her. He dodged round another tree and thrust out an arm to encircle her waist. His hold was steel hard and inescapable and it brought her to a standstill, breathing shortly and struggling to escape while he hung on to her determinedly.

'Keep still!' he ordered sharply. 'Stop it, Laurie!'

'Let me go!'

He merely put a firm hand on each of her arms and turned her round to face him, still keeping his hold on her. 'Now keep still, and stop behaving like a wild thing,' he told her.

'You have no right——' she began, and he shook her. Not hard, but hard enough to make her gasp.

'Stop arguing and listen to me for a minute, will you?'

'I—I don't have to listen to you,' she told him breathlessly, and he shook his head, a trace of the old familiar smile on his face.

'Nevertheless you're going to,' he informed her.

She glared at him resentfully, her eyes dark with anger and frustration. 'You're hurting my arms,' she told him. 'And my bruises might be as hard to explain as Mrs. McAdam's.'

He chuckled, not altogether surprisingly, and eased his grip slightly. '*Touché,*' he said.

Laurie lifted her chin and looked down her nose at him. 'If I'm supposed to be the—the wild woman of the glen,' she said, 'aren't you afraid of being out here alone with me? I might hit *you* on the head with something.'

He laughed and shook his head. 'I don't think so,' he told her. 'Although you'll probably slap my face given half a chance, that's why I'm hanging on to you.'

'I'd like nothing better,' she agreed tartly, and he laughed again.

There was, she thought, both amusement and speculation in his eyes when he looked down at her and she wondered what was going on in his mind now. 'Do I gather from that crack you made just now that you know about the stately home business?' he asked, apparently discarding the matter of his ex-sister-in-law for the moment.

Laurie nodded warily. 'Grandpa told me about it last night,' she said. 'And I didn't have to be told whose idea it was either. Although Grandpa tried to defend you.'

He regarded her quizzically. 'Grandpa would,' he

said. 'But you, of course, would have absolutely no doubt it was my idea, right?'

'Of course it is,' she insisted with absolute confidence.

'I see.'

'Well, it *couldn't* be Rod,' she told him, and he cocked a brow at her curiously.

'Why not?'

She blinked at him for a second time, then frowned. 'Of course it couldn't,' she told him. 'You said yourself that Rod's a romantic—he wouldn't dream of turning that beautiful old house into a—a public exhibition.'

She disliked the sarcastic-looking smile that tilted one corner of his mouth and made him look a little cruel. 'No, of course not.'

Laurie ignored the sarcasm and set about driving home her last point in favour of it being him and no one else. 'And I don't believe Russ would be so—so insensitive as to think up a scheme like that,' she told him.

'I see.'

'So that leaves you,' Laurie informed him triumphantly, and he laughed.

'And of me you can believe anything, is that the idea?'

'More or less,' she agreed, her chin in the air, daring him to deny it.

For a moment he said nothing, but his eyes held hers and there was a strange, unfathomable look in them that made her uneasy. More exasperation than temper, she thought, but there was something else too, something she could not recognise.

'All right, damn you,' he said at last, with quiet vehemence. 'If that's how you feel, you're entitled to your opinion—but then so am I.'

She looked startled for a moment, then bit her lip anxiously when she recalled the original subject of their encounter, and the reason she had walked off and left him. 'You—you can't really believe that I—I attacked Mrs. McAdam,' she said, her heart thudding anxiously again when she thought of the possible consequences. 'You know I couldn't, Quin.'

He flicked a doubting eyebrow. 'No?'

She held his gaze uneasily. Suppose they were all of the same mind, and chose to believe Rose McAdam instead of her? After all, they had known Rose for much longer than they had known her, and Rose was still, in a way, family.

'Quin, you can't!'

'I don't see *why* I can't,' he said quietly. 'But it isn't me who matters, is it, Laurie?' There was a hint of unholy glee in his eyes for her discomfiture. 'It's Rose who could call in the law and have you locked up for assault and battery.'

'Oh no!' She put her hands to her mouth and looked at him over the tops of her fingers, her eyes huge. 'Is that what——' She swallowed hard, and blinked reproachfully when he laughed.

'Oh, don't worry,' he told her. 'I talked her out of it. They won't be leading you away in handcuffs yet awhile.'

'*You* talked her out of?' Laurie asked curiously, and realised even as she spoke that he was probably the only one of them who could have done it.

He nodded, smiling wryly. 'Yes, fortunately I'm a better advocate on your behalf than I am on my own.'

She did not question his meaning but looked down at a place somewhere in the region of the breast pocket of his shirt. 'Thank you,' she said meekly. It was difficult to know just what to say in the circumstances, especially when she was still uncertain whether he believed in her innocence or not.

'Don't mention it.'

Laurie hesitated, anxious that at least one of the family should be fully convinced. Then she looked at him steadily, wishing her voice sounded less husky and uncertain. 'Quin, I *did*n't do it, really, please believe me. I found her there unconscious and with that bump on her head, just as I said. Either Suli must have thrown her or—or a low branch caught her and knocked her off but I *did*n't hit her, truly.'

He too hesitated briefly, then put out a hand and gently touched her cheek, so gently that a shiver slid along her spine and she felt like crying again. 'I believe you,' he told her. 'If I hadn't been pretty sure, I wouldn't have bothered talking Rose out of having you locked up.'

They stood there for a moment, still and silent and Laurie could almost hear the rapid thudding of the pulse in her forehead. Then he glanced at his wristwatch, and cocked a brow at her enquiringly.

'Hadn't you better go and get some work done soon?' he asked. 'Or Russ will think you're not coming in this morning.'

She hesitated, unwilling to face anyone else until

she knew for certain whether or not they suspected her of attacking Rose McAdam. In fact she panicked at the very idea of Russ believing that she had been responsible for his ex-wife's condition, and her feeling showed in her face.

'I'm—I'm not sure I can face Russ,' she said at last, and he lifted her chin with one hand, smiling slowly at her lowered gaze and the wary, half-scared look on her face.

'Scared?' he challenged softly, and she nodded.

'I don't know what—what he might think,' she explained, fervently wishing she was not such a coward.

'He doesn't think any worse than I do,' he assured her. 'And you'd be playing right into Rose's hands, you know, if you stay away today.'

She looked up then, her eyes huge, vulnerable and appealing. 'Quin——'

'Would you feel better if I came and held your hand?' he suggested, and she hesitated again. 'Come on, Laurie. Where's the fighting spirit of the Blairs?'

'It must be missing in me,' she told him, and he shook his head firmly.

'Not on your life,' he argued. 'Not when you're ready to take me on the way you do. If you can tackle me, you can face Russ, he's not nearly such a so-and-so as I am.'

She laughed at that, and already felt better, nodding her head. 'I have to agree with you there,' she told him.

'Sweet child!' he retorted. 'You don't need anyone to hold your hand, you little wretch, least of all me.'

Laurie shook her head, looking appealing again. 'I—

I wish you would, Quin, please,' she said. 'I'm not very happy about seeing Russ, in case he——' She shook her head. 'I'd be very grateful if you *would* hold my hand.'

He smiled down at her. 'Literally?' he challenged, and she nodded, feeling a lot better when his strong fingers curled over hers and held them tightly as they walked back through the trees to the drive.

The moment was less embarrassing than Laurie had expected, but it had helped having Quin there too, although she could see that his presence puzzled Russ. It was largely due, she insisted later, to Russ's kindness and understanding, which had smoothed the way for her.

He said nothing about the incident, nor even about her being late, but it was evident from his manner that he had formed his own opinion and decided on her innocence, as Quin had done.

She did not see Rod until midday when she was returning after lunch and he looked uncommonly solemn when he saw her, taking her two hands in his in a gesture that looked as if it was designed to defy any-one who dared to criticise her. A rather dramatised gesture, as so many of Rod's were.

'You poor darling,' he sympathised, kissing her gently on her cheek. 'What you must have been through!'

Laurie looked a little taken aback at such extravagance. 'I haven't really been through anything at all,' she told him with a smile.

'But to have young Colin make that hoo-ha about you and Rose,' he insisted. 'It must be discomfiting for you, love.'

'Not really,' Laurie insisted. 'Russ hasn't said a word, and Quin was soon straightened, once I'd told him what happened.'

He looked at her curiously. 'Do you mean to say he actually had the nerve to tackle you with it?' he asked, and she shrugged uneasily, remembering the ensuing argument.

'Not exactly,' she demurred. 'He just dropped a few hints and I'm afraid I lost my temper with him. But I don't think he really believed I attacked Rose. In fact he said he didn't.'

'It would serve her right if you had,' Rod declared. 'She's been asking for it, the way she talks to you.'

Laurie looked at him uncertainly. 'Rod, you don't think I did it, do you?' she asked.

He kissed her long and lingeringly. 'Darling Laurie,' he declared earnestly. 'Don't worry about it any more. Whether you clobbered Rose or not is a matter of complete indifference to me.'

'Well, it isn't to me,' Laurie retorted, not at all sure that blind support, whether she was guilty or not, was quite what she wanted. It would have been much more satisfactory if he had stated firmly that he thought she had not done it.

'I'm sorry.'

She stood at the foot of the front steps with him, vowing not to be too long, so that she could make up some of the time she had lost in the morning. But Rod's attitude puzzled her and she studied his good-looking face for a moment from under her lashes.

'Rod, you don't really think I did it, do you?' she asked, and he put his arms round her and hugged her.

'Darling, I've told you, I don't care whether you did or did not.'

Laurie frowned. 'That's not what I asked you,' she said, and he kissed her lightly on her brow.

'Well, don't look so worried, sweetheart. It'll be all right, you'll see.' He smiled then, and raised a brow, looking at her with that look that always reminded her of Quin. 'Just as a matter of interest,' he said, '*did* you hit her?'

'Rod!' She glared at him indignantly. 'I did *not*!' She pushed away the arms that held her. 'I knew you were blaming me,' she told him, bitterly disappointed. 'You of all people!'

He looked so very contrite that she knew she would not stay angry with him for very long. 'Oh, Laurie,' he said penitently, 'I really am sorry if I've upset you.' She looked up at him from under her lashes, reproachful still. 'Please forgive me?' The plea was irresistible, and she suspected he knew it.

'All right,' she told him with a rueful smile. 'I'll forgive you, though I don't know that I should.'

He kissed her again, much more in earnest this time, and for much longer so that she was not only breathless but on tenterhooks in case anyone, Quin in particular, came out and caught them. 'You're very beautiful and very forgiving,' he told her when at last he released her.

'I'm not always forgiving,' she told him, remembering what else she had discussed with Quin. 'I shall never forgive Quin for having that ghastly idea about opening Clach Aros to the public, and I've told him so.'

'You've heard about that?' he asked, and she nodded.

112

'Grandpa told me last night—I expect he got it from Quin.'

She thought he looked at her a little uncertainly for a moment, then he dropped another kiss on her nose and pulled her close to him so that his chin rested on the top of her head. 'Is making Clach Aros a stately home the unforgivable sin?' he asked, and she nodded, as best she could.

'It is to me, I'm afraid,' she said. 'I hate to think of hordes of strangers tramping round the old house, and I think Quin is unfeeling and insensitive to suggest it.'

'Did he tell you it was his idea?' Rod asked, and she shrugged.

'Not in so many words,' she admitted. 'But he didn't deny it either, and anyway I'd have known it was him. He's the only one who'd think of such a thing for Clach Aros.'

He laughed, a little uneasily, she thought. 'Condemned out of hand,' he said lightly. 'Poor old Quin!'

'Don't you think he deserves to be condemned?' she demanded, and he nodded hastily.

'Oh yes, every time,' he agreed.

'I knew it couldn't be you or Russ,' she told him. 'So it had to be Quin.'

'The Philistine of the trio?' he suggested lightly, and she smiled.

'Something like that, I suppose,' she agreed, though not quite sure she would have gone that far. Then she raised her head just far enough to plant a kiss on his chin. 'Anyway, I'm very glad it isn't you,' she told him. 'I couldn't imagine myself misjudging anyone as completely as that.'

He said nothing, but hugged her close again and rested his chin on the softness of her hair. So it was that Quin found them when he came down the steps a few minutes later, and Laurie pushed Rod away with both hands. That knowing smile was on Quin's face again, and she hated it.

'Sorry to break up love's young dream,' he teased, and tapped Rod on the shoulder with one hand. 'Come on, kid brother, duty calls.'

Rod's good-looking face flushed bright pink at the jibe, and he glared at Quin resentfully. 'Don't talk down to me, Quin,' he told his brother. 'I don't like it.'

'Sorry, old son.' Quin's expression showed neither regret nor resentment, but he looked at Laurie with a speculative eye. 'How's it been this morning, Laurie?' he asked. 'No backlash yet?'

'None at all,' she told him, haughty on Rod's behalf. 'But then I didn't expect anything unpleasant from Russ.'

He cocked a doubtful brow at her. 'No?' he said softly. 'That wasn't the impression you gave this morning. You wanted me to hold your hand, remember?'

Laurie glanced hastily at Rod and met a curious and not altogether approving look, wondering if Quin had been deliberately provocative, and if so, why. 'That was only—figuratively,' she said, and was treated to that rising brow again and the sight of a gleam of unholy glee in his eyes as he looked at her and dared her to deny it.

'It felt like a real hand I held when we came back here,' he told her solemnly, and Laurie hastily lowered her eyes against the challenge.

'I—I was nervous about facing Russ this morning,' she said, for Rod's benefit entirely, and he looked at her as if he expected a full explanation, and nothing less. 'I saw Quin and—and——'

'—l I gave her a third degree to find out if she really had gone for Rose with that stick, as Colin said,' Quin intervened. 'She convinced me she hadn't and we walked back here together—end of episode.'

He made it sound much more simple than in fact it had been, Laurie thought, but she had no intention of denying any of it, and Rod was already looking better pleased about things. 'Oh, I see,' he said. 'In other words she put you firmly in your place, is that it?'

Quin smiled wryly. 'You could say that,' he agreed, and only his eyes, relentlessly fixed on Laurie, betrayed his amusement at the idea.

CHAPTER SEVEN

LAURIE had quite expected Rod to be somewhere in the vicinity of the stable when she went to fetch Brownie, but he was nowhere to be seen. It was Saturday afternoon and he usually joined her for a ride on Saturdays, unless he was wanted for some chore around the estate, usually one designated by Quin.

Apparently he was wanted today and had already gone out, for she noticed that both Quin's grey and Rod's Arab were missing from their stalls. Obviously he was out somewhere with Quin on estate business, and she swallowed her disappointment and resigned herself to riding alone.

During the past few days she had denied herself the pleasure of riding because she was frankly unwilling to face Rose McAdam again since her accident and the ensuing accusations against herself. She seldom saw her during working hours, but Rose McAdam also rode and it was possible she might bump into her if she came to the stable, so, until today, she had stayed away.

She knew that the other woman was fully recovered from her accident and was up and about again, because Rod had told her so. He had also said that she showed no sign of leaving yet, much to his regret, and Laurie wondered how much longer the visit was going to be

extended.

There was no doubt that Russ enjoyed having his son with him, even though it involved having to tolerate his mother being there as well, and if only she had been prepared to stay at the hotel and not keep visiting the house, it would have been better for everyone. But while Quin was such an attraction Rose McAdam was unlikely to either stay away from the house or leave altogether.

It was such a pity, Laurie thought, that Russ could not spend more time with the boy. He was much less able to be a constant companion to him than most fathers were because of his disablement, and Laurie felt deeply for him having to watch Colin go off riding or walking without him.

She knew it must pain him more than he would ever admit, for she had seen the hurt look in his eyes when the boy rode off with Quin or, very occasionally, with Rod. He seemed a sensitive, thoughtful boy, however, and he quite often spent time with his father when he would probably have preferred to be out of doors. For that Laurie could forgive him a lot—even his wild accusations against herself after his mother's accident.

Of his two uncles he seemed to prefer Quin, a choice which rather puzzled Laurie, because she would have thought their characters far too different for there to have been any rapport between them. Quin too seemed fond of the boy, but it was possible, of course, that he was more attracted to his brother's ex-wife than he allowed anyone to know, and that his affection for Colin stemmed from an affection for his mother.

She pondered that question as she rode Brownie out

of the stable yard and skirted the trees, heading for the open moor. As far as she knew there was no legal impediment to a man marrying his brother's divorced wife, but if Quin McAdam did have that in mind then it was taking him a long time to come to the point.

It was four years since the divorce and Rose Mc-Adam was a determined woman, so it could not be for want of encouragement. More likely, she guessed, it was because of the embarrassment it could cause them all with the two brothers working so closely together.

She decided to ride out towards Killie Sloc for a change today and enjoy the warm breeze that tempered another hot, sunny day. There were no clouds holding a threat of rain today, only a clear sweep of bright summer blue overhead and shimmering round the distant hills like a vast swathe of bright silk.

The hills themselves glistened hazily in the heat, and looked to be even closer than usual. But Laurie knew that distance could be very deceptive in such conditions and instead of allowing herself to be lured by them she made her objective a small dark tree-filled hollow that lay about half-way between Clach Aros and the hills.

When she reached Killie Sloc old Margaret Mc-Kinnon would almost certainly ask her in for a cup of tea and some of her delicious little honey cakes. She smiled to herself at the thought of those honey cakes, a favourite since childhood, and clucked her tongue softly at Brownie, urging her along a little faster.

It was several weeks since she had seen old Margaret. Not since she and her grandfather had moved out of Clach Aros had she ridden this way, and for a moment her courage failed her. Old Margaret had known her since she was a tiny child and she had always been the young lady at 'the house'.

When she was very small she had called her wee Laurie, but never since her teens. She had become Miss Laurie then and treated with the same respect her grandfather commanded. It was going to be very difficult now that their circumstances were not so very much better than their former tenants'.

It was doubtful if Margaret McKinnon had even absorbed the full meaning of the change yet, Laurie thought. Angus McKinnon had loved and worked on the Blair estate for all his grown life, and when he died his widow had been allowed to stay on in the tiny cottage. Such generous gestures had helped, in part, to undermine the financial strength of the estate, but Laurie could not find it in her heart to blame her grandfather.

Old Margaret, however, would probably find it difficult to realise that the Blairs were no longer her landlords, for she was nearly ninety years old and did not take kindly to new ways. It was worth a moment to wonder how she had greeted Quin McAdam on his first visit to her.

That he would have called on her, Laurie had no doubt, for he had very properly called on all their tenants when they took over the estate. It gave her a moment's satisfaction to imagine old Margaret's indignant reaction to his arrogance.

The tiny cottage stood right at the edge of Killie Sloc, and long before she reached it Laurie could see its neat, whitewashed walls standing out starkly against the dark green of the backing trees. Brownie was familiar with the sight of it too, and she hastened her pace without encouragement at the prospect of sugar lumps and cool, sweet water from the burn.

It seemed like a lifetime ago when she had last come out here, Laurie thought, and shook her head over the prospect of explaining the passage of events to the old woman.

Her welcome was as warm as she had expected, and the old woman clasped both her hands in her own gnarled ones, her incredibly wrinkled face creasing further into smiles of welcome. 'Come away in,' she bade Laurie, in her soft, gentle voice, still retaining a hold on one of her hands even while she led the way into the one small living-room the cottage possessed.

It was spick and span and shiny as a new pin, as it always was, and the old woman murmured soft words of welcome and endearment in the Gaelic as she signed Laurie to the best chair. It would not have done for Laurie to refuse, even though her instincts prompted her to, for the old woman was very proper in her proto-col and would have been only shocked and uneasy if their positions had been reversed.

'It's lovely to see you again, Mrs. McKinnon,' Laurie told her, raising her voice to make herself heard. 'It seems such a long time since I was here last.'

' 'Tis too long by far,' the old woman agreed. 'Ye'll take some tea, Miss Laurie?'

'Thank you, I'd love some,' Laurie smiled, her wish granted. She dared not offer to help either, but instead stayed in her chair and talked to her hostess as she prepared them tea. 'There's a lot happened since I was here last,' she went on, wondering just how much the old woman knew.

'Aye, I heard.' The old lady shook her head slowly, in genuine regret.

'You—you know we had to sell Clach Aros?'

Mrs. McKinnon nodded. 'I heard,' she said. 'An' 'twas a sad day, Miss Laurie. Sad indeed when a family like the Blairs have to give up their home an' all.'

'We—we miss it terribly,' Laurie told her, glad to unburden herself to someone who would understand.

For a moment the bright old eyes, much less effective than they looked, studied her gravely. 'I heard you were grievin' badly over it too, Miss Laurie,' she said, her soft voice almost bringing Laurie to tears.

'I—I am,' Laurie admitted. 'At least, I'm getting a little more used to it now.'

Margaret McKinnon nodded. She had the gift of making folk talk, Laurie remembered, and she would have liked nothing better than to tell the old woman everything about the McAdams, and all the things that had been troubling her for the past couple of months.

'I heard, though,' old Margaret went on in her soft, persuasive voice, 'that Mr. Blair himself is bearin' up well, an' takin' the changes much better than yeself, Miss Laurie.'

'You heard that?' She stared for a moment, knowing it must have been Quin who had told her so much, for as far as she knew her grandfather had not visited the cottage since their move. But it was not easy to imagine Quin being persuaded to say so much, even to such a gifted listener as Margaret McKinnon.

When Laurie looked at her again, the old eyes held a surprising hint of mischief as she looked over one shoulder. 'Mr. McAdam told me about it,' she informed her, and Laurie frowned.

'I expected he would have been to see you,' she said.

'He came an' saw me an' told me all about the way it was with you,' she told her.

Her lack of any show of anger or indignation came as a shock to Laurie and she looked at the old lady curiously as she set out her best cups and saucers. 'You mean Quin McAdam, of course?' she guessed, wondering if by any chance Rod had been delegated to visit her instead, but the old lady was nodding her head.

'Mr. Quinton McAdam,' she agreed precisely. 'A very pleasant young man.'

'You liked him?' Laurie had a nasty sinking feeling in the pit of her stomach when she saw yet another should-be ally lost to Quin's dubious charm.

'Indeed I did,' Mrs. McKinnon assured her. 'He was so sympathetic about takin' the house an' all.'

So sympathetic, Laurie thought bitterly, that he's now trying to turn it into a tourist sight. 'Was he?' she said.

'Much better to have a man like that in the house, Miss Laurie,' her hostess told her gravely, 'than one o' those foreign people who'd not know the way to treat a place like Clach Aros.'

The temptation to tell her the plans for the house was there, but Laurie resisted it, partly because she could not give Quin the satisfaction of accusing her of gossiping. 'I'm glad *you* like him,' was all she said.

'He's a gentleman,' old Margaret informed her with an air of one who knows what she is talking about. 'A fine gentleman like Mr. Blair himself, an' I'm glad that the two of them are good friends.'

So he had even told her that, Laurie thought wryly. He had missed out nothing. 'I—I suppose you know that we live in the lodge now?' Laurie ventured, watching her pour boiling water into the teapot, and the old lady nodded sadly, as she put tiny honey cakes on to a plate and set them on the table.

'Aye, I heard,' she said. 'But there's worse places, I dare say, an' mebbe it'll not be for too long.' She glanced at her shrewdly as she poured out their tea. 'Ye're workin' for the new laird, are ye not, Miss Laurie?'

'I'm working for one of them,' Laurie allowed, seeing that no stone had been left unturned. 'There are three of them, you know.'

'Aye.' The neat white head nodded wisely. 'Ye still have yon wee mare, I see,' she added, and Laurie detected a hint of curiosity in her voice.

'Yes, I have,' she agreed. 'At least, they allow me to take her out sometimes. I don't own her now.'

'No matter,' the old woman told her. ' 'Tis another good sign.'

'Oh?' Laurie eyed her curiously. 'Do you know something I don't, Mrs. McKinnon? You made a remark just now that maybe we wouldn't be in the lodge for very long.'

'Aye, well, mebbe ye won't,' Mrs. McKinnon said knowingly.

'I—I don't understand you.' It was too much to

hope that there was something, some hope, that they would be able to go back to Clach Aros. Perhaps her grandfather and Quin had produced a solution that she knew nothing about.

The old woman stirred her tea and smiled gently. 'Marriages have saved many a fortune, Miss Laurie,' she said softly. 'An' there's a fine, handsome young man with no wife an' just waitin' for the right woman.'

'Mrs. McKinnon!'

Laurie stared at her, remembering the mischievous look she had surprised earlier. It was not only the idea itself that stunned her either, but the possibility that the old woman had mentioned something along the same lines to Quin while he was there.

Margaret McKinnon could see nothing wrong in marrying simply to regain possession of what was rightly hers, and the fact that Quin McAdam was an attractive man would merely make the proposition even more desirable. But Laurie could only think of how she could possibly face him again after this.

'You—you didn't say anything like that to Mr. McAdam, did you?' she asked, praying the answer would be no.

'Och, now don't ye fash yesel', Miss Laurie,' she soothed. 'He'd not take notice of an old woman's ramblings, even if I had.'

'But you didn't, did you?'

'No, no—though I did ask if his wife liked the country.'

'You're an incorrigible matchmaker, Mrs. McKinnon!' Laurie scolded her, smiling despite her own apprehension. 'You always were, so Grandpa said.'

The old woman was offering cakes, a small gentle smile on her face, but keeping her eyes downcast, perhaps because she detected a note of disapproval in Laurie's voice. 'Ah, there now, mebbe I was,' she admitted. 'But it would be a fine thing, would it not?' she added softly. 'For you ta marry the new laird.'

'It would not,' Laurie declared firmly, biting into a cake and savouring its wonderful sweetness for a moment before continuing her argument. 'For one thing,' she went on, 'Mr. McAdam and I very seldom see eye to eye on anything.'

The neat white head nodded understanding. 'He'll be a man who knows his own mind, I don't doubt,' she said with some satisfaction.

'He's arrogant and unfeeling,' Laurie insisted, uncaring that she was maligning her hostess's new landlord. 'I could no more marry Quin McAdam than— than—fly to the moon,' she finished, somewhat lamely she had to admit, in view of recent events.

'Aye weel——' Another little smile doubted the finality of the statement. 'He's a braw man for a' that, an' he's a man tae get what he wants, I've nae doubt.'

Laurie did not question the meaning of her last words, for she thought the conversation had gone quite far enough along those lines. She had come to Killie Sloc expecting to find old Margaret McKinnon mourning the changing ownership of Clach Aros and indignantly refusing to recognise the new laird.

Instead, while she was certainly in sympathy with their predicament, she was far from condemning Quin McAdam as the heartless, arrogant cause of their humiliation and was even bent on marrying her off to

125

him. Like her grandfather, she seemed to like the interloper and made her feel as if she was being unreasonable because she didn't.

Laurie had left the cottage at Killie Sloc with an uneasy heart. No one, it seemed, was prepared to see her point of view with regard to Quin McAdam, and she foresaw a lonely battle against him in the future if she was to save Clach Aros from being a public showplace. If everyone was so ready to fall in with his plans, it was obvious that they would fall in with anything he might propose for Clach Aros, and the idea gave her a sudden feeling of loneliness.

She wished Rod was with her, for then she felt she would have had an ally. He was fond of his brother, but not blind to his faults, and, while they had never actually said much on the subject of Clach Aros's proposed new role, she still felt sure that he would be on her side and dislike the idea intensely.

What she must now try and do, she thought, was to seek his firm support and try and persuade him that, no matter how Quin pushed the idea, he must stand firm and refuse to lend it his support. They were all equal partners, she knew, and probably if Rod refused, Russ would allow his finer feelings to prevail as well, and not allow himself to be bulldozed into supporting Quin.

It was with that prospect firmly cut and dried in her mind that she turned Brownie towards home and gently urged her on faster. She was within half a mile of Clach Aros when she saw two riders coming from the direction of Glen Cummin, and looked forward to meeting with Rod. The two horses were easily recognisable and so was the rider of the grey, but it was not Rod who was riding Suli, the black Arab. It was, she suspected, Rose McAdam.

She was herself spotted at almost the same instant and Quin raised a hand in greeting. Tempted to ignore it, she eventually waved a hand, confounding the luck that had brought Rose McAdam across her path after all, and especially in company with Quin. He would probably find some kind of confrontation between Rose McAdam and herself quite amusing, she thought, although her conscience reminded her that it had been he who had persuaded Rose not to take her accusations any further.

Laurie had no desire to come into any closer contact with either of them, and she put her heels to Brownie, hoping to be back and unsaddled before they arrived. It was rather a vain hope, but worth a try, she thought, and urged Brownie on to greater efforts. She had no doubt at all that had Quin been alone he would have given chase and caught up with her, but his companion would have no such desire, and they were soon left behind her.

She unsaddled Brownie and rubbed her down carefully, seeing her settled contentedly in her stall, then she turned to leave and almost bumped into Quin with the other two horses just coming into the stable. She had been so lost in thought that she had heard nothing of their approach, and she let out a startled gasp when she almost collided with him, her eyes round and surprised and her lips parted.

'Hello!' he grinned, still blocking her way out. 'Are you still bent on running away?' She looked behind him and the two horses, and he laughed. 'It's all right,' he assured her. 'Rose went into the house.'

That at least was a relief, she thought, but she still bit her lip anxiously. It was quite ridiculous, of course, but suddenly old Margaret McKinnon's drastic solution for getting back Clach Aros kept coming to the forefront of her mind, and she could not help wondering whether she had said more than she admitted to Laurie about it.

Laurie hastily lowered her eyes when he held her gaze for too long, but not before she had been made discomfitingly aware of the half amused look in his eyes and the intriguing way dozens of tiny lines crinkled at the corners of them when he smiled.

'I'm sorry,' she said hastily, and stepped back. 'I'm blocking your way.'

'In a hurry to escape as usual,' he guessed, leading his two charges in, and turned to smile at her over his shoulder. 'You're always in a hurry to leave when you see me, aren't you, Laurie?'

'No—no, of course I'm not,' she denied, and was startled at the way her heart reacted when he laughed softly.

'Good, then perhaps you'll give me a hand, will you?'

'Yes, yes, of course.'

'You take Hamish,' he told her, handing over the grey. 'And make sure he doesn't bully you—he will if you let him.'

She led the big grey into his stall warily, and took off his saddle, finding it just about as high as she could reach as she hauled the heavy thing from his back.

Hamish shifted, anxious to be free of it, and she let out a small squeal of surprise when the unexpected move put her off balance and landed her face down between his feet, the saddle wedged uncomfortably underneath her.

'Laurie, what——'

Quin came round the edge of the stall and grabbed her hastily from between the grey's restless hooves, pushing her back against the side of the stall. 'Are you all right?' he asked, and when she nodded, lifted her chin with one hand and looked down at her. 'You're sure?'

'Yes, yes, I'm perfectly all right, thank you.'

'That's O.K., then.' He gave her a long hard look for a moment before bending to recover the saddle from the floor. 'What happened?' he asked a moment later, and Laurie shrugged, brushing straw and clinging pieces of hay from her clothes.

'I was off balance and he moved,' she told him shortly.

Quin hung up the saddle, then came back and stood looking at her for a moment in silence, a smile tilting his wide mouth at one corner. 'It was my fault,' he said. 'I forgot what a midget you are. I shouldn't have asked you to do it.'

'I could have managed perfectly well,' Laurie protested, feeling as if she was being treated rather like a child who has been given a task just beyond her capabilities.

'But you fell flat on your face, and I'm sorry.'

'You don't have to be,' she insisted. 'If he hadn't moved unexpectedly I could have managed quite well.'

He grinned, looking at the big grey, looming beside them. 'He could have eaten you for lunch,' he said. 'I should have realised you couldn't reach properly.'

Laurie glowered at him. 'He's *not* too big for me to handle,' she argued. 'And I wish you'd stop talking to me as if I was a sweet little five-year-old!'

'Holy mackerel!' Quin breathed piously. 'You're not a *sweet* little anything, my child. I never saw such a snappy little devil in my life. What gets into you, Laurie? Are you always so determinedly bad-tempered, or am I singled out for the iceberg treatment?'

'I don't——' she began, but he took her arm firmly and drew her out of the cramped confines of the stall, still retaining his hold on her even when she was leaned against the rough stone wall of the stable.

'And don't bother to deny it,' he told her brusquely. 'I'm getting a little tired of being treated as if I had the plague. I suppose I've inadvertently trodden on your sensitive toes again, although I'm damned if I know how or when, so suppose you tell me.' Laurie did not answer, but her pulses were racing wildly as she hazarded a guess at her chances of escape. 'Answer me!' He shook her by the arm he held, and there was an exasperated gleam in his eyes as he looked down at her.

'Don't *do* that!' She pulled at the captive arm and tried to free herself, but in vain.

'Laurie!'

'I don't *have* to explain my activities to you,' she retorted, disturbingly aware of how near he was, and that ridiculous suggestion of Margaret McKinnon's whirling persistently round and round in her brain.

'I'm not asking you to explain your activities to me,' he told her shortly. 'I just want to know why you're so damned unfriendly towards me, that's all, and I think I'm entitled to that.'

'You're not entitled to anything,' she denied. 'Now let me *go*!'

'Laurie! I warn you, I'm rapidly losing patience with you!'

If only she could have forgotten that idea of marrying him to get Clach Aros back she might have been prepared to call a truce, she thought, but suddenly she had a very real fear of actually liking the idea, and that was simply not to be considered.

'Very well!' His voice had an edge of hardness on it, and the icy look was in his eyes when he looked down at her. 'If you can't be reasonable about it, then you can damned well do without your privileges.'

'My—my privileges?' She raised her eyes and looked at him curiously and a little apprehensively.

He was smiling, but it was a tight, grim smile that owed little to humour. 'You can't expect to treat me as if I was the lowest form of life and still have things all your own way,' he told her. 'You won't take Brownie out again until I tell you you can.'

Laurie stared at him for a moment, unwilling to believe she had heard him aright. 'But—but you wouldn't,' she said huskily, and he looked down at her steadily.

'I would,' he declared flatly. 'I have.'

'But the horses belong to—to all of you,' she insisted, refusing to recognise his right to deny her her favourite form of relaxation. 'You *can't* stop me if Rod

131

—or Russ, says I can ride.'

She knew from the tight-lipped way he was smiling that the answer was one she wouldn't like, and she looked down at the spot where his open-necked shirt showed a vee of tanned throat, and waited. 'The horses are nothing to do with the business,' he informed her. 'In everything else we're equal partners, but the horses are different. Suli belongs to Rod, but Hamish and Brownie belong to me. So you can cancel out all the devious little plots you're planning for rolling your eyes at one or other of my brothers. If *I* say you don't ride, you don't, my girl, it's as simple as that.'

'You—you brute! You selfish, egotistical brute!' Laurie declared, her eyes glowing darkly blue between their fringing lashes, and a bright spot of angry colour on each cheek. 'Just because you don't like being told that—that I object to you treating me like a—a five-year-old, you do a mean, selfish thing like that!'

He had a hand either side of her head, resting flat-palmed against the wall, and he leaned towards her, the ice-grey eyes glittering with an anger that matched her own. 'The way you go on,' he told her harshly, 'you'll be lucky I don't turn you over my knee and really treat you like a five-year-old.'

'You—you wouldn't dare!' she whispered, her eyes wide and fixed warily on his, not altogether sure that he wouldn't do just that.

'No?' He leaned a little closer and she felt his breath warm on her face when he spoke. 'You wouldn't care to pursue that *too* closely, would you, Laurie?'

'Quin!' She ducked down under his arm and he, rather surprisingly, chuckled as she moved away from

132

him as swiftly as possible, turning by Suli's stall to smile over her shoulder at him when another possibility occurred to her. 'You don't own Suli,' she reminded him. 'I'll get Rod to let me ride *him*.'

For a brief moment she thought she saw a hint of anxiety in his eyes, then he shook his head and smiled. 'Rod's got more sense than to let you,' he said.

'I don't see where sense comes into it,' she retorted. 'Rose—Mrs. McAdam rides Suli.'

'And gets thrown,' he reminded her. 'And you're a different proposition from Rose anyway. She's bigger, taller and stronger than you. Suli would make mincemeant of you in no time at all.'

'There you go again,' Laurie complained indignantly. 'I'm a perfectly capable rider, and Rod knows I am.'

'If Rod lets you talk him into it,' he threatened, 'I'll personally break his neck before Suli breaks yours. You stay away from that black-hided devil, Laurie, or I'll——'

'You'll what?' Laurie challenged, and laughed at his black frown.

'Laurie!'

She turned in the stable doorway and smiled her triumph at him. 'Rod'll listen to me,' she assured him, confident she was right. 'And there's nothing you can do about it.'

CHAPTER EIGHT

IT was nearly a week since Laurie had been riding, and she was even more bitterly disappointed because Rod would not let her ride Suli. 'It's too risky,' he told her for the hundredth time as they sat on the garden wall one lunch-time.

'Who for?' Laurie retorted. 'You or me?'

'Why, you, of course,' Rod said uneasily. 'I don't understand——'

Laurie laughed shortly and looked down her nose at him. 'You're as much afraid of what Quin will say to you as of what might happen to me,' she accused, and almost immediately felt sorry because he looked so hurt.

'Oh, darling Laurie, that simply isn't true,' he protested.

'Then will you let me ride Suli?'

He looked very much like Quin for a brief moment when exasperation showed in his eyes, then he put out his hands and gently placed them either side of her face, leaning towards her so that he spoke close to her mouth. 'I can't, Laurie.'

'Because you're afraid of Quin?'

He sighed and kissed her before answering. 'Because I'd never forgive myself if anything happened to you, my sweet. I'd willingly *let* Quin break my neck, as he's threatened, if I was ever foolish enough to let you ride Suli and he threw you like he did Rose.'

She smiled up into the dreamy grey eyes so close to her own. 'Oh, so you *do* believe he threw her?' she said softly.

'Of course.'

'There's no of course about it,' Laurie retorted, still smiling. 'You were quite prepared to believe that I'd hit her over the head with a club the last time we mentioned it.'

'Ah well, now I know better.' He kissed her again, less gently this time, and pulled her close into his arms. His arms were strong and he held her so tightly she could scarcely breathe, let alone move. And there was nothing dreamy or poetic about the way he was kissing her either, so that her heart was skipping rapidly against her ribs.

'Rod!'

When he released her mouth it was only to kiss her with equal ardour on her neck and forehead and the smooth, pulsing spot at the base of her throat, his voice muffled in the thick softness of her hair when he spoke.

'Oh, Laurie, Laurie!'

She was horribly uncertain whether she was enjoying his obvious ardour or not, and she did little to encourage him. Not, she thought, that he needed encouragement. 'Rod, please——'

'Please be nice to me,' he begged huskily. 'And please don't ask me to do something I know I'll be sorry for.'

She put her hands against his chest and pushed him

135

away far enough to enable her to look up into his eyes. They looked much darker than usual and glowed with a warmth and excitement that did crazy things to her pulse, and she shook her head to try and clear it of the thousand and one impulsive things that raced through her brain.

'Are you *still* afraid of what Quin will say?' she said, and he shook his head.

'You don't know him like I do,' he told her. 'He really *would* break my neck if I let you have Suli and anything happened to you.'

'Oh, nonsense, of course he wouldn't. He'd simply say it served me right and probably have a good laugh, then forget all about it.'

Rod looked down at her solemnly, shaking his head slowly. 'You really *don't* know him,' he told her.

'But he——' She hastily shook her head and lowered her eyes because the things that were going around in her mind were not only crazy but highly improbable. She took a deep breath and laughed, a short, nervous sound, and rather breathless. 'Well, it's really up to you, of course,' she told him. 'If you don't want me to have Suli, I won't try to persuade you any more.' Then she looked up at him again, the heavy lashes half lowered over her deep blue eyes. 'Only it's very bad for my morale,' she added, 'when you resist my powers of persuasion so easily.'

'Laurie!' His arms tightened round her when she tried to free herself.

'I'm disappointed,' she told him, her mouth pouted reproachfully. 'And I told Quin you *would* let me— now he's got something else to crow about.'

For a moment he looked at her steadily, and she could almost imagine the battle that was going on inside him as he fought against his wariness of doing anything to displease Quin. Then he nodded, pulling a face before bending his head to kiss her again. 'All right,' he sighed resignedly.

'You mean—I can?' She lifted her face after a second and kissed his chin. 'Oh, Rod, you're wonderful!'

'I'm asking for trouble,' he said ruefully, 'and I shouldn't be doing it.'

'I'm glad you are.'

'But I'm coming with you,' he told her. 'And I'm getting Brownie for you, not Suli.'

'But you can't,' Laurie protested. 'If Quin knows——?'

'He needn't know if I'm careful,' Rod said. 'But we shall have to be a bit cunning about it.'

'How?' She was beginning to feel as if she was taking part in some fantastic intrigue.

'I'll have to think.' He sighed deeply. 'I don't know what Quin's going to say, but I've promised, so we'll go.'

Laurie hugged him, well satisfied now that she was to be mobile again, and gratified too that he was prepared to brave Quin's inevitable wrath for her. 'Can we go this evening?' she asked.

'I don't see why not, though I'll have to be very careful sneaking Brownie out, because if he sees me, he'll stop me taking her.'

'Oh, it'll be all right,' she assured him, more con-

137

fident every minute. 'And thank you a thousand times, Rod.'

'I do miss my rides with you,' he confessed. 'And Quin had no real right to stop you using Brownie.'

'Except that he likes to boss,' Laurie observed dryly.

He looked down at her curiously. 'Why *did* he stop you?' he asked.

Laurie shrugged, unwilling to go too deeply into that. 'Oh, just one of his fits of bossiness,' she said airily, and Rod did not press the point, to her relief. 'When and where shall I see you this evening?'

He frowned over it for a moment. 'It's essential that he doesn't see *you* anywhere near the stable,' he said, and pondered further. 'Mm. Yes, I know how we can do it. I'll bring Suli down to your place before Quin gets back tonight.'

'Suli? But I thought——'

A raised hand silenced her and was alarmingly reminiscent of Quin. 'If he notices Suli is gone, he'll only conclude that I'm out, or possibly Rose,' he explained. 'If he sees Brownie isn't there he might get suspicious, especially if Colin's here at the house. So I'll leave Suli at your place, then sneak Brownie out when I get through with Russ. O.K.?'

'Fine,' she said, willing to agree to anything that would allow her to go riding again. 'I'll wait for you by Cummin Rock. It'll be better if I go as far away as possible from the house and I can manage Suli that little way.'

'Well, don't go any further,' he admonished, again with more than a hint of Quin in his manner. 'I'll be there about seven.'

She smiled up at him, well pleased with her victory. 'Thank you, Rod.' She tiptoed and lightly kissed his mouth. 'I'll see you at seven.'

'Before that,' he reminded her. 'I'm with Russ this afternoon, thank heaven.'

Laurie glanced hastily at her wristwatch and pulled a face. 'So am I,' she said. 'And I'm going to be late if I don't go right now.'

He kissed her gently on her mouth, looking very solemn. 'Laurie.' She smiled enquiringly, hoping he wasn't having second thoughts. 'Please wait for me to bring Brownie for you. Suli really is hard to handle, and I'd never forgive myself if *you* were thrown like Rose.'

'I won't be,' she assured him, then frowned curiously when she remembered something he had said earlier. 'Just out of curiosity,' she said, 'why are you so suddenly sure that Rose *was* thrown?'

He shrugged. 'Quin,' he said shortly.

'Quin?' Her frown deepened and for the moment she forgot that she was on her way back to start work again. 'What does that mean?' she asked, and he shrugged his shoulders again.

'He got the truth out of Rose,' he told her, almost reluctantly. 'He made her admit that Suli had run away with her and that she was knocked off her seat by a low branch. She admitted that you had nothing to do with it.'

'Oh—oh, I see.' For a moment she was unsure just what her feelings were at the news. Certainly it was a relief to know that there was no longer any shadow of doubt in the matter, but it disturbed her too, in some

139

strange way, to think that Quin had taken so much
trouble to clear her. And his doing so could have done
nothing to endear her to Rose McAdam, she felt sure.
Even Rod seemed oddly reluctant to admit that his
brother had gone to such lengths for someone he pro-
fessed to have little time for.

'Rose hated admitting it,' Rod told her. 'But you
know Quin when he puts his mind to anything.'

'Yes,' Laurie said softly, as she turned to go back
to the house. 'Yes, I think I do.'

It had seemed a very long afternoon to Laurie, but
she knew it was only because she was so looking forward to going out that evening. Although once or twice
when she had looked at Rod, busy at Russ's desk, she
wondered from his expression if he was having second
thoughts.

She missed her rides more than she would have
believed possible and the past few days without her
daily outing with Brownie had given her some idea of
what it would have been like if Quin had not made that
original generous gesture and allowed her the use of
the mare.

How long it would be before he relented from his
present edict she had no idea, but she had found herself once or twice during the afternoon, toying with the
idea of trying the same tactics with him that had
worked so well with Rod. She had hastily dismissed
them, of course, for one thing because he would be
much less susceptible than Rod, and for another because she was strangely shy about using her femininity
to persuade Quin. The result, she felt, could be so

140

much more disturbing.

She cooked dinner for herself and her grandfather and tried not to notice the way he looked at her curiously while she busied herself in the kitchen. 'What are you up to?' he asked suddenly, as she sat down at the table, and Laurie blinked for a moment in surprise.

'What do you mean?' she asked.

'I mean,' her grandfather told her patiently, 'that you and Rod McAdam are up to something, and I'm curious to know what it is.'

'Oh well, it's nothing very criminal,' she assured him with a smile, although it made her uneasy to remember how friendly he was with Quin. 'We're going for a ride, that's all.'

'Oh?' The old man regarded her for a moment while he helped himself to vegetables. 'I thought Quin had put a stop to your riding for the moment. Has he relented?'

'No, he hasn't,' Laurie retorted, knowing he was going to disapprove of their plan. 'Quin isn't the type to relent.'

'Then how,' her grandfather asked, 'are you going to ride?'

Laurie did not look at him, but concentrated on her meal, her eyes carefully downcast. 'Oh, Rod's organising it,' she told him airily.

The old man nodded. 'And I suppose the fact that there's been a familiar and very beautiful black Arab gelding in our back garden for most of the afternoon had nothing to do with it?' he suggested.

'Well—yes, in a way.'

Her grandfather's shrewd old eyes watched her

141

across the table for a moment. 'You're not thinking of riding him, I hope,' he said then, and she shook her head.

'No—no, Rod's—Rod's bringing Brownie down for me.'

'Without Quin's knowledge?'

She nodded, feeling suddenly less excited about the prospect of her ride, and rather as if she was doing something mean and underhand. 'It—it'll only be for a little while, Grandpa,' she said. 'He won't know.'

'And that makes it right?'

'Well—no. No, I suppose it doesn't, but—oh, I don't know—it seemed a good idea at the time.' She was already feeling very guilty about it and wished she had never agreed to the idea of sneaking Brownie out of her stall. It would have been simpler if Rod had just let her ride Suli, then she wouldn't have been answerable to Quin at all.

'It's Quin's animal, isn't it?' her grandfather asked, and she nodded.

'Yes.'

'But you're prepared to take it without his consent?'

'Oh, you make it sound as if we're—I'm stealing it,' she cried. 'We're—we're only borrowing her, that's all, and if he hadn't been so mean and unreasonable it wouldn't have been necessary.'

'Just why did he stop you?' he asked, as Rod had done, and she was no more willing to answer him than she had been Rod.

'Didn't he tell you?' she retorted, and he simply looked at her steadily. 'I'm sorry, Grandpa, but—well, you know how unreasonable Quin can be.'

'I know how unreasonable *you* say he can be,' he told her quietly. 'Just what happened this time?'

'He—he says I treat him as if he has the plague,' she admitted, quoting Quin himself, and she saw a small tight smile at the corners of the old man's mouth as he cut into his dinner carefully.

'I think perhaps you do,' he told her, and Laurie looked at him reproachfully.

'I can't help it if I don't like him,' she said defensively. 'He always makes me feel——' She shrugged uneasily, unable to explain exactly how Quin did make her feel. 'I don't know—small.' She sought for the right words, her meal forgotten for the moment. 'He talks to me as if I was a child, and it makes me so mad I just automatically hit back.'

'Not literally, I hope,' her grandfather said quietly, with surprising facetiousness.

'I did once,' Laurie admitted. 'And I'm not sorry either.'

The old man raised a brow at her briefly. 'You surprise me,' he said. 'That Quin let you get away with it.'

'He didn't exactly.' He had, she remembered only too well, left her stranded on the moor and then, inexplicably, come back for her. There was a great deal about Quin McAdam that was inexplicable, she thought.

The old man cocked a curious brow at her. 'I thought it didn't sound like Quin to let you get away with anything,' he said, and his evident satisfaction made her frown.

'Quin McAdam,' she said firmly and with absolute

143

conviction, 'is a bully and a—an egotistical monster.'

'Quin McAdam,' her grandfather argued quietly, 'is a strong-minded, very virile man, and the sooner you recognise it the better you'll get on with him.'

'I've no desire to get on with him,' Laurie declared. 'I don't like him, and it isn't really very important one way or the other whether I do or not. I work for Russ, and I ride with Rod, I don't have to have anything to do with Quin at all.'

'You do if you want to ride his horse,' her grandfather reminded her, and she looked at him reproachfully.

'You *would* be on his side,' she accused. 'You're as thick as thieves, Grandpa, and I don't think it's fair.'

'Why?' He ate his meal unconcernedly, and Laurie realised with a start that there were a lot of characteristics in common between Quin McAdam and her grandfather.

'Because you should be on my side,' she told him. 'Instead you always think *he's* right and I'm wrong.'

'Oh, not always,' he denied, and she could have sworn he was laughing at her.

He said no more on the subject of Quin, but had it not been for a streak of stubbornness that refused to allow her to back down, Laurie would have called off the ride she had worked so hard to get. As it was she cleared away and washed up, then went upstairs to change, leaving her grandfather sitting behind a daily newspaper, puffing away at an old pipe.

'Laurie—visitor!' She was just going into her bedroom when her grandfather's voice called her from downstairs and she glanced at her watch with a puzzled frown. If it was Rod, he was very early, unless something unforeseen had forced him to change his plans. 'Your escort's here,' her grandfather informed her, and she shrugged her shoulders and changed direction.

'I'm coming!' She went downstairs, still wearing the short, pretty cotton frock she had worn all day, a smile in readiness for Rod when she opened the sitting-room door, then stopped and stared open-mouthed at Quin.

'Surprised?' he asked quietly, a hint of iciness in his eyes, although he looked faintly amused at her expression.

'I—I was expecting Rod,' she said huskily.

As if he wouldn't know already, she thought bitterly a moment later. It was obvious that Rod's plans had gone awry and she felt guilty for his sake, because it would have been Rod that caught the full weight of Quin's anger in the first instance and he would never have done anything at all if it had not been for her.

'So I gathered,' he told her.

Her grandfather, she noticed with dismay, had disappeared into the nether regions of the cottage and left her to face the music alone. Quin stood by the window, dressed as he usually was in slim-fitting light trousers and an open shirt, his fair head slightly untidy, probably where he had run his fingers through it, and he looked almost overpoweringly big in the tiny cottage room.

'Where—where is he?' she asked, and he cocked a brow at her.

'At home, nursing his pride.'

She looked at him fiercely, guessing how Rod must

be feeling. 'Oh, you shouldn't have blamed Rod,' she told him. 'It wasn't his fault at all.'

'I know exactly where the blame lies,' he told her quietly, his gaze steady and infinitely disturbing. 'That's why I'm here.'

'Oh, I see.' She shifted uneasily, not quite knowing what to say. 'Well, I'm glad you realise it wasn't Rod.'

'It was Rod I caught horse-stealing,' he said, and she thought he was serious. 'They used to hang horse-thieves, you know.'

'And you wish they still did, no doubt,' Laurie retorted before she stopped to think.

The ice-grey eyes held hers steadily for as long as she could stand it. 'You can never resist getting at me, can you, Laurie?'

She said nothing for a moment, but felt utterly miserable because suddenly everything seemed to have gone wrong, and not only was she to be deprived of her ride but she had got Rod into trouble as well. 'What—what did you say to Rod?' she asked meekly.

He was in no mood to relent, obviously, for there was no relaxing of the stern air and he looked down at her as if she had committed the unforgivable sin. 'It doesn't concern you what I said to Rod,' he told her, and would have gone on, but she looked at him angrily, her blue eyes dark and shiny with tears of frustration.

'It does concern me,' she told him. 'I happen to be very fond of Rod, and it wasn't his fault any of this happened. *I'm* to blame and you should take it out on me, not Rod.'

One brow cocked speculatively and there was a glimmer of the old familiar expression in the half smile.

'You're rather inviting trouble, aren't you?' he asked softly. 'Just what do you suggest I do to extract revenge?'

'I——' She raised her eyes and looked at him, at a loss to know how to answer. 'I don't know,' she said at last. 'But I'm sorry.'

'Because you planned to take Brownie without my knowing, or because you were caught at it?' he asked, and immediately shook his head before she could object. 'I shouldn't have said that, Laurie,' he told her, surprisingly. 'I'm sorry.'

Laurie turned away from him, looking utterly despondent. 'Oh, I suppose you have every right to be sarcastic,' she allowed, with unexpected meekness. 'We—I shouldn't even have thought of taking Brownie without your permission, but——' She looked over one shoulder at him wistfully, for a moment, her eyes big and appealing. 'I *do* miss my rides,' she said.

He said nothing for a moment, then he reached out with one hand and touched her cheek. It was a gesture so light and gentle that she instinctively leaned her face against his hand for a brief second, a shiver running down her spine like a trickle of ice.

'Then there's nothing I can do but let you *have* your rides, is there?' he said softly, and Laurie gazed at him for a moment or two, unbelievingly.

'You—you mean you'll let me have Brownie again?' she asked huskily.

He studied her face for a moment, with only a hint of laughter in his eyes. 'Well, you don't think I'll allow you to ride Suli, do you?' he asked.

She still did not move, but looked at him wide-eyed,

trying to make up her mind what could possibly have prompted his sudden and unexpected change of mind. She had expected anger, and he had definitely been angry initially, but this sudden relenting was not only unexpected but very disturbing.

'I—I thought you were—were angry,' she said, unable still, to grasp his mood.

'So I am,' he informed her, 'but since your daily ride is so important to you that you're prepared to resort to cloak-and-dagger tactics with Rod, you'd better have your way.'

'I—I don't know what to say.'

'Thank you, Quin?' he suggested mildly, and she smiled.

'Thank you, Quin,' she echoed obediently.

For a moment he stood looking at her, and there was some expression in his eyes that set her pulses racing and gave her a strangely reckless feeling that she fought hard to control. 'I wasn't too hard on Rod,' he told her softly at last. 'I know just what he was up against, but do me a favour, will you, Laurie?'

She gazed at him questioningly. 'Yes, yes, of course, if I can.'

'I'd rather you didn't use your *femme fatale* tactics on Rod again,' he said, with every appearance of being serious. 'He's far too susceptible, and heaven knows what you'll get him into next. If you want to practice on anybody—try it on me.'

Laurie glanced up at him through her lashes, a small provocative smile coming unbidden to her mouth. 'That would be rather a waste of time,' she said.

'Exactly,' he agreed. 'That's the idea.'

It was not the answer she had expected and she pouted reproachfully—something else that she realised was a waste of time. 'I—I suppose Rod will be on his guard against my—my wicked wiles from now on, thanks to you,' she guessed, and he grinned down at her.

'That's right,' he agreed. 'I think he's got cold feet for the moment.'

'So you did bully him!' The retort was impulsive, and she wondered for a moment if she had spoiled everything again, but he was still smiling.

'Right again,' he said. 'And if you don't watch your p's and q's, I'll bully you too.'

She eyed him for a moment, speculatively, then thought better of the retort she had in mind. 'Poor Rod,' was all she said, instead.

'Poor Rod?' He cocked a brow and she saw that strangely disturbing look in his eyes again. 'I don't feel sorry for him at all. Not when he has so much going for him.'

'He has you bullying him,' Laurie retorted, and he laughed.

'And you consoling him,' he said softly. 'That's worth any amount of bullying, Laurie.'

Again that wildly racing pulse in her forehead made her feel lightheaded, and she held his gaze for a long moment, before sweeping her lashes down to hide her eyes. 'I—I really am grateful to you for letting me have Brownie again,' she said huskily. 'I won't go tonight, not now, but I'll be out tomorrow morning, like I used to be.'

Again he was silent for a disturbingly long time,

and when she looked up at him again he moved away from the window and stood so close to her that she could feel the warmth and strength that emanated from him. One finger traced the curve of her cheek and he was smiling.

'Lucky Rod,' he said softly, and his fair head bent over her slowly until his mouth was just a breath away from hers. She lifted her face to him and her eyes were already half closed when the kitchen door opened and her grandfather walked in.

'Ah,' he said with unaccustomed facetiousness, 'I thought it had gone very quiet.'

CHAPTER NINE

DESPITE the fact that it had been a fairly showery day, the evening was fine and bright, with only small feathery clouds to be seen, although beyond the hills it looked darker and more menacing, as if there was still a promise of rain to come by nightfall.

Laurie thought she could afford to ignore it, however, for she would be back long before it reached the lower ground. She was riding alone this evening, because Rod had come to tell her that he would be busy with some chore that Quin had found for him at the last minute. Not that she really minded, for she could enjoy her own company quite often.

Rod had ridden with her every evening since she had been allowed the use of Brownie again, and she strongly suspected that Quin had thought it time he pulled a little more weight. She smiled in sympathy with Rod, but would not allow it to spoil her own pleasure, no matter how selfish it might make her seem.

A light wind had cleared the air of the day's sultriness, and blew refreshingly on her face as she took Brownie down the slope towards the loch. The water looked darker and deeper than it sometimes did in summer, and its surface was ruffled with the light wind, so that its character was quite different from the smooth, placid mirror it had been the last time she had seen it.

She kept Brownie to a slow enough pace for her to enjoy the scenery, relaxing in the stillness and the peace that surrounded her. The distant hills were girdled with mist this evening and appeared to shift slightly with every breath of wind that stirred the trailing mist.

The sky, a pale greeny-blue, seemed to hang low and spattered little shadows over the surface of the loch when the clouds drifted by. It had a smooth, painted look that changed colour with every second. It was evenings like this, Laurie thought, that made her thankful to be still at Clach Aros, even in her present circumstances.

Just back from the bank of the loch she dismounted and left the patient Brownie standing with her head bowed contentedly to the cool touch of the turf on her sensitive nose. Even Brownie enjoyed such moments as this in her own way, and would wait patiently enough.

Laurie walked right to the water's edge and stood on the flat grey stones that formed a rim round the sides, a tiny figure in the vastness of her surroundings. She bent and picked up a handful of white pebbles from near her feet and began, languidly, to throw them one after the other into the deep, rippling water.

She found satisfaction and complete absorbtion in watching the concentric circles that spread out towards her, and noticed nothing else until she heard the sound of someone approaching—someone on horseback.

There was no mistaking the sound—the occasional

click of iron shoes on the flinty stones, and she frowned her dislike at the prospect of being disturbed. Even Rod would be unwelcome at the moment, for she was enjoying her peaceful solitude and had no wish to have it broken into.

She feigned ignorance of the impending arrival for as long as she could by keeping her back turned and carrying on with her stone-throwing. But she could not hope to get away with such obvious tactics for very long, and she sighed almost audibly when someone spoke from just behind her.

'Hello, Laurie.'

She turned reluctantly and was not altogether surprised to discover that it was Quin and not Rod who had joined her. He had left the big grey standing beside his stablemate and stood beside her at the water's edge, smiling at her. He was curious, she could see that, but in the brief look she ventured at him she saw the inevitable gleam of amusement in his eyes too.

'Hello,' she said, not very encouragingly, and turned back to send more pebbles plopping into the water. If she did not particularly want to see Rod at this moment, she certainly did not want a verbal battle with Quin, and inevitably it would come to that if he stayed.

'Something wrong?' he asked, confirming her guess that he was curious.

'No.'

'Somebody upset you?'

'No.'

He laughed shortly. 'I see, just feeling unsociable, huh?' He bent and gathered himself a handful of pebbles. 'You haven't fallen out with Rod, have you?'

153

he asked.

'No.'

He sighed, then sent a pebble skimming across the surface of the water. 'You seem to be stuck in a mono-syllabic rut,' he told her. 'And it isn't Rod's fault you had to come out alone tonight, you know.'

'I know that,' she told him shortly.

'I had to give him a last-minute job to do, I'm afraid.'

'Of course you did,' Laurie said.

'Sarky!'

She glanced at him briefly. 'Well, I'd have known it was *you* who found him a last-minute job to do, even if Rod hadn't told me, because Russ doesn't do things like that.'

'Oh no, of course he doesn't,' he agreed wryly.

'Anyway, I don't mind being alone sometimes,' she told him. 'In fact I quite enjoy being alone.' It was as broad a hint as it was possible to make and he chuckled deeply when he recognised it.

'Well, if you don't mind being alone, and you're not out with Rod,' he said, 'what *is* causing the sulks?'

'I am *not* sulking!' She turned an indignant gaze on him, her blue eyes sparkling. 'You would think that, wouldn't you?'

'Oh, inevitably,' he agreed, but sounded very uncon-cerned about it. 'I automatically think the worst about you, as you do about me.' It was a jibe she could not argue with, but she pouted her dislike of it. 'We're a bit like chalk and cheese, aren't we, Laurie?'

'Yes, we are,' she agreed, and could not imagine why she sounded so much as if she regretted it.

'Never a dull moment,' he went on.

'It isn't *my* fault,' Laurie denied hastily, and he chuckled again.

'You're not standing where I am!'

'Well, it *isn't*,' she insisted, seeing her peace well and truly shattered now. 'We—we just never see eye to eye, that's all.'

'Does it bother you?'

She glanced up hastily at him, puzzled by something in his voice, and saw that strange, disturbing look in his eyes again, so that she quickly looked away.

'Not really,' she told him, her eyes following the progress of another pebble as he hurled it far out over the water.

He said nothing for a moment, then a hand slid under her arm and half turned her towards him. 'We could call a truce,' he suggested.

Laurie gave it a moment's thought. He *had* come down to the cottage to see her, prepared to lay down the law, but then he had said she could have Brownie again, just when she had thought he was absolutely adamant about stopping her from riding.

He was a difficult man to understand, and she was not at all sure that she would ever understand him, but there seemed no real reason why she was being so unfriendly towards him at the moment.

'I—I rather thought we *had* a truce,' she ventured then, and looked up again briefly.

She felt a shudder of something course down her spine like icy water when she met his eyes, and saw that same curiously intent look she had seen in them just before he had so nearly kissed her at the cottage the other night—before her grandfather interrupted.

'So we have,' he said softly, as if he too was remembering.

'I—I'm sorry, Quin.'

He tightened the hold he still had on her arm, and shook his head. 'What for?' he asked.

'For snapping at you.'

He smiled slowly. 'I've already forgotten,' he told her.

'I just felt like being alone for a while, that's all.'

'We all do at times,' he said quietly.

'You too?' She looked up at him and the fingers on her arm squeezed gently.

'Me too. Shall I go away again, or may I stay and enjoy some of your peace?'

She nodded, realising as she spoke that what she was saying was only too true. 'It's your peace really, isn't it?' she said, looking round at the loch and the familiar beauty of the moor. 'It's all yours now.'

'And it still hurts?'

She nodded. 'Sometimes more than others,' she admitted, and he smiled understanding.

'And that's when you hate me most,' he guessed.

'I don't——' she began, and looked up swiftly to deny it, but then just as hastily looked away again, shrugging off the mood of self-pity that was fast catching up with her, and the fingers squeezed her arm again.

'I'm glad,' he said softly.

She sought rapidly for a safer subject, her mind whirling crazily in all directions at once. 'I—I was thinking of going a bit further afield, if I had time,' she told him.

'As far as the river, for instance?' he suggested, and smiled when she looked at him in a way that betrayed how accurately he had guessed.

'I had thought of the river, yes.'

'Then let's go, shall we?'

She had not anticipated having his company, but she could not very well refuse it, and she was not even sure that she wanted to, so she nodded, moving over to the two waiting horses.

The river was quite a bit further on and away to the west, but there was plenty of time before it became too dark. It seemed she was not the only one given to acting impulsively that evening either, for he too seemed to be acting on impulse. He helped her to mount, and then swung himself up into the saddle, bringing the grey alongside her, so close that they almost touched, and Hamish tossed his head at the proximity of his stablemate.

'O.K.?' Quin asked, and for answer Laurie merely nodded and put her heels to Brownie.

The big grey was much more difficult to hold at the pace set by the more easy-going Brownie. He tossed his head and snorted impatiently, and only the firm hand on the rein stopped him from taking matters into his own hands.

'Hold it, Hamish!' his rider admonished him. 'Behave yourself when you're with a lady!'

Laurie could not resist a smile at the reprimand, and he grinned at her amiably. 'Hamish is a man's horse,' he told her. 'He hasn't very good manners in mixed company, but he's a good mount, and a stayer, which is what I need.'

'He's enormous,' Laurie observed. 'And much too strong for me, I expect.'

He glanced at her sharply. 'He most certainly is, and don't you get trying to prove otherwise!'

Laurie lowered her eyes in mock humility. 'I wouldn't dream of doing so, without your permission,' she told him.

'No,' he observed dryly, 'I'll bet you wouldn't, given half a chance.'

She looked at him from under her lashes, judging his reaction to her next statement. 'I'm going to ride Suli one day,' she told him. 'Rod says I can.'

He laughed shortly. 'Rod'll let you do anything if you open your big blue eyes at him,' he said.

Laurie stuck out her chin, on the defensive again. 'I can manage him,' she retorted, and Quin smiled dryly.

'Rod—or the horse?'

She raised her chin and tossed back her hair, both gestures of defiance. It looked as if they were drifting back on to familiar ground again. 'Both, if necessary,' she told him, and he shook his head in warning.

'You might wind Rod round your little finger,' he told her, 'but if I ever catch you trying to ride anything but Brownie or something equally manageable by somebody your half-pint size, I'll personally see that you don't feel like sitting a horse again for several weeks!'

'You——'

He ignored the attempted objection and went on relentlessly. 'Your grandpa's too old to keep you in order, but he trusts me to keep an eye on you.'

Laurie's face was flushed a bright rosy pink and her

eyes sparkled like jewels. So much for their truce, she thought bitterly. He could not resist treating her like a child that was incapable of taking care of itself. It was obviously no use at all trying to meet him on equal terms, he just would not relinquish his big brother attitude, and no matter what right he thought he had to treat Rod that way, it certainly did not apply to her. With or without her grandfather's approval.

'Will you stop talking down to me?' she said shortly. 'If you don't, I shall do something drastic to you, Quin, I swear I will!'

It did nothing for her dignity when he took in her flushed face and slight figure in one brief, swift appraising glance, then grinned. 'Oh yes?' he said.

'Don't think that just because you can bully Rod into being scared of you, that you can do the same to me. No matter what Grandpa says or thinks, I'm a grown woman and I'll not be treated like a—a baby by you or anyone else!'

'No?'

'No!'

'That was quite a little speech,' he remarked blithely. 'Do you often get on your soapbox like that?'

'It's *not* funny, Quin!' Funny or not, he laughed softly to himself, and Laurie glared at him. 'Calling a truce with you is a complete waste of time,' she informed him, and put her nose in the air haughtily, determined to ignore him.

She was so exasperated with him that she did not even take much notice of the familiar and breath-catching scenery around them, but rode with her face turned sternly forward, her eyes sparkling with anger.

She could, she supposed, have turned around and ridden off without him, but until it was too late, the idea did not even occur to her.

They had been travelling downhill for much of the time and were rapidly approaching the river, with its great grey boulders standing up like bulky sentinels, thrusting their way through the turf and heather, and giving the place an air of slightly unreal grandeur that the lowering sun emphasised. It was a beautiful spot and one of Laurie's favourites, although she did not come here as often now as she had once done. Perhaps because it was a much longer ride than going to the loch and she had less time for riding.

The river itself was audible as they came nearer. Splashing and sparkling over its rocky bed, its edges frothed and frilled with creamy foam created by its headlong rush as it sped its way westward. The sun, lower in the sky now, gave it the look of deep gold, as if it was indeed molten metal and not deep water, a look that was somehow awe-inspiring however many times one saw it.

It was a sight she had not seen for some time and Laurie's temper evaporated in the beauty of it. It was so long since she had stood here on the banks and seen the river turn to gold, and she was glad she had come, even if it was in the company of Quin McAdam. Perhaps *because* she was in his company, because there was something of her own reaction reflected in his eyes too.

'Oh, it's so beautiful!' she breathed softly as they dismounted and went to stand almost at the very edge of the bank. 'I'd almost forgotten just how beautiful it was.'

He stood close beside her, watching the rapid, deep water flow past them, and his hand touched her arm lightly, as if he feared she might go too close to the edge. 'And how dangerous?' he said quietly.

She did not shake her arm free of his hold, but glanced at him over her shoulder. 'I know just how dangerous it is,' she told him. 'I've been here often before.'

He smiled. 'Good,' he said quietly. 'As long as you know what you're about, then I shan't have to jump in and pull you out.'

She turned again and looked at him curiously, a disturbing and rapid pulse tapping away at her temple as she held his gaze. '*Would* you jump in and pull me out?' she asked.

There was that disturbingly intense look in his eyes again when he smiled. 'Why not?' he asked. 'Don't you think I would?'

'I—I don't know.' She lowered her eyes at last, and looked at the swift flowing water. 'You might think it was a very good opportunity of getting rid of a thorn in your flesh.'

'I might,' he agreed gravely, and she flicked him a brief suspicious glance. 'But I'm strongly anti-pollution,' he added with a grin, 'and I don't somehow think you'd do the fish in the river very much good.'

'Oh, you——!' To her surprise she found herself with an irresistible urge to laugh, and after a moment or two she could resist it no longer and she threw back her head and laughed unrestrainedly.

She was still laughing a moment later when his

161

hands gripped her arms tightly and pulled her to him, so close that she could see the fine lines at the corners of his eyes and the warmth in them when he looked down at her mouth intently. There was a taut excitement about him that matched her own as, for a long moment, he held her there in silence.

'You should laugh more often,' he told her huskily then, his words warm against her lips.

She could feel the rapid, dizzying thud of her own heart and the strong, steadier beat of his as his face came down closer, and she tipped back her head. Then his mouth closed firmly on hers and she felt herself being whirled along lightheadedly, as if she would never touch ground again.

'Quin!' She spoke indistinctly against his ear as he buried his face in the thick darkness of her hair, his lips warm on her neck and throat as he held her irresistibly tight and with an urgency that at once both alarmed and excited her.

'Quin!' Another, harsher voice echoed her whisper, and brought Laurie swiftly back to reality.

She freed herself from Quin's strong hands and moved away from him instinctively, turning to meet the blazing malice in Rose McAdam's eyes. She was riding Suli and the thin, bony hands were gripped tight on the Arab's rein, as if it served to hold back her anger too.

'Hello, Rose.' Quin sounded quite unconcerned at her arrival.

'You could have waited for me,' Rose told him, her voice taut and harsh, but still hanging on desperately to her temper.

Quin shrugged, his smile doing nothing to placate the other woman, as Laurie realised. 'I didn't know you were coming out,' he told her off-handedly.

'You could have asked.'

Laurie, in a brief wary glance, saw his brows draw closer in a hint of frown. Surely, she thought, Rose McAdam should have known her ex-brother-in-law better than that. He disliked nothing more than being put at fault, and most especially by a woman.

'I had other things on my mind,' he informed her shortly, and she tightened her already thin lips.

'Obviously,' she said tartly. 'I saw you from some distance off, and I guessed it was you.'

'So you thought you'd come too,' Quin guessed quietly, an unfamiliar hardness in his voice which the newcomer either did not notice or chose to ignore.

'Do you mind?' she asked, and Quin shrugged.

The hard, unfriendly blue eyes turned on Laurie again and there was no mistaking her feelings at finding her there with Quin. No doubt too, she had witnessed that altogether unexpected and very disturbing kiss. What was puzzling Laurie at the moment was whether or not Quin had seen her coming and had, yet again, deliberately acted as he did to provoke the other woman. If he had, Laurie thought wildly, she would never, ever forgive him again.

'You have a bad memory, *Miss* Blair,' Rose McAdam told her harshly, evidently referring to her previous warning about her and Quin.

Laurie flushed, biting on her lip not to be equally acid in return, but she had no desire to indulge in a slanging match for Quin's probable amusement. 'I should be getting back,' she said with what she considered was admirable restraint.

Quin moved across towards their horses too, but Laurie's withdrawal was blocked by her antagonist and she could only reach Brownie by going right round behind her. Before she could take more than one short step, however, the Arab leapt forward sharply and without warning and she was knocked off her feet.

She heard Quin's voice, vaguely, as she fell backwards, and the high, excited whinnying of the black gelding, then the cold, swift-flowing water closed over her and she momentarily lost consciousness as she went under.

The river was deep and there was far less handhold on the rocks than there appeared to be when she tried to catch hold of them after her first, breathless ducking. The water was unbelievably cold as she struggled to gain a hold, her breathing short and painful.

'Quin!' Her cry was instinctive and she knew he was there in the water almost as soon as she was herself, strong hands holding on to her tightly as he fought against the surging speed of the river.

'All right, all right.' He spoke quietly, but she heard it above the sound of the water and hung on to the rock he guided her to. 'Get you breath back,' he told her, still supporting her. 'O.K.?'

She nodded, her wet hair falling over her face and into her eyes, one cheek grazed on the rock as she fell. 'I—I'm all right,' she assured him through chattering teeth, and was not really surprised when she saw the brief glimpse of a smile.

'Then hang on tight and try to stay upright.'

They were only a few feet from the bank, but gaining it was not easy for the depth and swiftness of the water, so that they were both breathing heavily when at last Quin climbed out and reached down to haul her up beside him.

Laurie lay flat on her face for several moments, feeling as if her lungs would burst, her head spinning crazily, then she was lifted and turned over so that she looked up into Quin's face. The ice-grey eyes looked dark and anxious and he was not smiling now but breathing heavily as he looked down at her.

'Thank you,' was all she said, and her voice was choked and husky with the water she had swallowed.

'You're all right?'

She nodded, trying to sit upright, although he still kept one arm round her. 'I'm—I'm perfectly all right.' She looked at him, dripping wet and looking suddenly older with deeper, craggier lines round his mouth and eyes so that the deeply tanned face had an almost primitive look as it looked down at her. 'Are *you*?' she asked.

After a brief hesitation he grinned, running his fingers through the thick wet hair over his forehead. 'Like you, I'm a bit wet, but nothing worse.'

Laurie looked across the moor to where the silky black Arab was flying over the turf with Rose McAdam using her heels to drive him yet faster, anger and frustration in every line of her slim body. 'She's gone,' Laurie said simply, and he nodded.

'Now I must get you home before you catch pneumonia.'

'What about you?' she asked, already on the defensive at his protective air.

He grinned. 'I'm tough,' he told her, standing up and reaching down for her hands. 'But as stand-in grandpa for you, I'd better see you come to no harm or I'll have the real Grandpa on my trail.'

'You're not my keeper,' she told him, but smiled as she said it. Somehow it was amusing having him as a substitute grandfather and she must make the most of it.

He was unrolling a waterproof jacket from the saddle and he draped it round her while Laurie tried to evade it. 'I'm your keeper for the time being,' he told her. 'And why you always have to be soaking wet when I rescue you after Rose's ministrations I don't know! Now put your arms in this jacket, Laurie, and don't go awkward on me, I'm in no mood to argue.'

'Then——'

'Put it on, damn you!' He grabbed her arms one at a time and pushed them into the jacket sleeves, then zipped it up to under her chin. 'Now come on, get aboard and I'll get you home and dry.'

Obediently she allowed him to help her mount, then nodded when he asked if she was all right to ride. 'I'm perfectly all right,' she told him. 'I'm much tougher than I look, you know.'

He grinned across at her as he swung himself up, shaking water from his hair. 'I doubt it,' he told her. 'Now get a move on before something else happens.'

Brownie had seldom gone so fast for so long, but Quin was relentless in his urge for speed and the little mare complied gallantly, stretching herself to the full across the open moor, while Laurie fought a growing

166

need to cry like a baby. It was reaction, of course, but by the time they got back to the lodge, the tears were rolling down her cheeks in dismal procession and she was crying quietly, biting her lip to try and stop herself.

There was no sign of her grandfather when they reined in just beside the cottage and Laurie wondered what he would have to say about this latest escapade. Although it was none of her doing. She could imagine what Rod's reaction would be and she wondered if it would precipitate a full-scale family row if he made his displeasure known to Rose McAdam. What Quin's attitude would be, she could not even guess. She had yet to decide whether or not he had kissed her on impulse, as she had first supposed, or whether he had seen Rose coming and done it deliberately to provoke her.

He came round to help her down and as he set her on her feet in front of him he saw the tears and the look of indecision in her eyes. 'Laurie!'

One finger gently touched her cheek and she sobbed uncontrollably at the gesture. 'I'm—I'm just—I'm just——'

'I know, I know.' Before she realised it, she was held tightly in his arms and her face pressed against the wetness of his shirt. 'You were frightened, my sweet love, and I should have realised it. I'm sorry.' He kissed her forehead lightly and then pressed her close to him again. 'Don't cry any more, it's all over.'

'Quin, I——'

He held her off from him for a moment, his eyes warm and gentle but showing a hint of their customary laughter for her bedraggled appearance. 'You look like a little water gypsy,' he told her softly, then laughed, shaking his head as if to dismiss the mood of gentleness. 'I don't know what Rod's going to have to say to this latest ducking you've had. You always seem to be getting drenched, don't you, and it's been my fault each time.'

'I'm glad you admit it,' she retorted swiftly and a little breathlessly. She was unsure whether to be angry with him about that endearment or just take it in her stride, but she definitely did not like the way he gave Rod the right to be proprietorial about her.

He laughed softly and slid his hands caressingly up and down her arms. 'I might as well,' he told her. 'Before you do.'

It was happening again, she thought wildly. They were gradually slipping back to normal, and she was oddly reluctant about it somehow. 'Quin——' She shook her head when he looked down at her enquiringly. 'I'd better go in and get these wet things off,' she told him. 'And so had you.'

She unzipped the jacket he had insisted on her wearing. 'You'd better have this back too.'

He helped her out of the wet sleeves and as it came free of her arms she glanced up at him, her pulses racing crazily when his hand brushed her neck. He said nothing, but after a brief, breathless second he dropped the jacket and pulled her suddenly into his arms, his mouth pressing down hard over hers, as if there was some desperate hunger in him.

Laurie had completely surrendered herself to the dizzying excitement of it and clung to him tightly when somewhere in the background she heard a familiar voice and brought herself reluctantly back to earth.

'*Now* what are you playing at?' Rod demanded, sounding more annoyed than surprised. 'Damn you, Quin, why can't you play fair?'

CHAPTER TEN

LAURIE looked at Rod uncertainly. It was going to be very difficult explaining it all to Rod without making much more of the incident than there need be. She had said very little last night when he caught her with Quin in what she had to admit was a rather compromising situation. Making the excuse that she was very wet and must change her clothes immediately, she had told him that she would see him tomorrow, and fled to her room. What explanation Quin had given him she had no idea. Probably none, since he seemed so curious now.

He looked less dreamily romantic than usual, she thought, as they strolled round the edge of the garden to the low wall where they invariably sat to talk. True, he was holding her hand, but he had made no attempt so far to make the contact more intimate, as he usually did, and she wondered just what he knew or suspected.

'Well, it seems you've succeeded in getting rid of Rose, anyway,' he told her.

She usually went riding with him on Saturday afternoon, but after last night's episode at the cottage she was unsure just what to expect, so she had not changed into riding clothes but merely walked up to the house in the offchance of seeing him.

He had not questioned her about it, but had kissed her briefly and suggested that they walk round the garden. She thought he looked more shrewd than usual too as he looked at her, and it crossed her mind that he was a lot more like Quin than she had realised.

'She's—she's gone?'

'Lock, stock and barrel,' Rod assured her. 'Early this morning.'

She glanced at him through her lashes, curious in her turn. 'It was rather sudden, wasn't it?' she asked, and Rod shrugged.

'Who cares? She's gone.'

Laurie was silent for a moment, wondering what could have prompted such a hasty withdrawal, and feeling vaguely uneasy, almost guilty. 'Well, I don't think I had anything to do with it,' she denied, and he looked down at her steadily, with eyes more like Quin's than their usual dreamy selves.

'Oh, but I'm sure you did,' he insisted. 'Judging by the bit I heard going on between Rose and Quin.'

She looked startled. 'You mean they were—they were quarrelling?'

Rod shrugged. 'You could call it that, I suppose, though it sounded more like Quin laying down the law, and eventually Rose apparently decided she hadn't a leg to stand on, and she went off with her tail between her legs.'

Laurie looked at him uneasily. Explanations, she supposed, were inevitable sooner or later, but she did not quite know how she was going to explain to Rod that when he caught Quin kissing her he was not the first one to see them that evening. It was possible, of course, that he knew all about how she came to be soaking wet, but somehow she did not see Quin going to the trouble of explaining.

'I suppose she's taken Colin with her too?' she said, and he nodded.

'Yes, that's the one drawback with her going. Poor old Russ misses Colin and she knows it, so she's bitch enough to take him with her, even though it's not him she's fighting with.'

'I'm sorry about Colin,' Laurie said, genuinely regretting it. 'I know how Russ will miss him.'

'*I'm* curious about what caused the fracas between Rose and Quin,' he said, returning to the matter in hand. 'I didn't overhear enough to get any more than the general gist of things. How did both you and Quin come to be soaking wet? Just what *did* happen, Laurie?'

She still hesitated. Explanations were inevitable, but she wondered how he was going to take the whole truth. He had been genuinely angry last night, she thought, but how much angrier was he going to be when he knew that kiss was not the first one that evening?

'I—I saw Quin down by the loch while I was out last night,' she began, and he laughed shortly, flopping down on to the low wall and pulling her down with him by the hand he held.

'Yes, after he'd taken care to give me a job to do to make sure I was safely out of the way,' he said.

'Oh no, Rod!' She looked at him uneasily. 'He—he wouldn't. I mean, not for the reason you're suggesting.'

'I wouldn't have thought so at one time,' Rod

admitted. 'But lately—I don't know, he's not running true to form. I've never known him comment on a woman's looks before, not out loud anyway, yet I've heard him do so a couple of times about you. Russ has noticed it too, and so, I might add, has Rose.'

'Oh, for heaven's sake,' Laurie said. 'That doesn't mean—I thought all men talked about that kind of thing among themselves.'

'Not all of them,' Rod demurred, his expression thoughtful.

Laurie found it hard to believe that Quin was un-interested in feminine company, and said as much. 'I can't believe Quin's never had a—a girl-friend,' she said, and Rod laughed.

'You're right, he's had more women friends than most, but he's never talked about them.' He pulled a rueful face. 'And I know my big brother, if he wants a thing, he'll stop at nothing to get it, even if it happens to be my girl.'

'Oh, Rod, you're wrong,' Laurie protested. 'And I'm not at all sure that I like being referred to as a thing, either.'

He squeezed her hand and smiled apologetically. 'It was just a figure of speech,' he told her.

'I still think you're wrong.'

She realised suddenly, however, that she did not know for sure if she was wrong or not. Quin was a very attractive man and he would certainly be aware of it. He would be ruthless too, she had said so herself, and if a particular woman took his eye she had no doubt he would resort to whatever means necessary to get what he wanted.

The only thing certain in her case, she felt, was that he did not think of her in that way. Granted those last two times he had kissed her had been something she could never forget, but apart from that his usual attitude towards her had scarcely been that of a lover. Even thinking of him in that light, however, brought a swift bright colour to her cheeks and she saw Rod's brow flick upwards in surprise when he noticed it.

'Suppose you tell me exactly what made Rose so mad,' he told her. 'And what made Quin tear into her like a wild thing when he came back here.' Laurie looked at him warily through her lashes and he smiled as he put an arm round her. 'I mean to know,' he told her, 'so you might just as well tell me, my sweet.'

Laurie pouted reproachfully at his tone. 'You,' she accused, 'sound exactly like Quin.'

'Then just pretend I am,' he said, 'and do as you're told.'

She traced the rough surface of the stone with the tip of one finger, and did not look at him while she spoke. 'I—I fell in the river,' she said, and again saw that doubting brow flick upwards.

'Fell?' he asked softly.

'Actually——' She hesitated. 'Rose rode your Suli straight at me, and knocked me in.'

For a moment he stared at her doubtfully. 'Do I need to ask why?' he asked softly, and she shook her head.

'It would have been enough that I was within half a mile of Quin,' she told him.

'It probably would,' he agreed. 'But was that the only reason, Laurie?'

174

She said nothing for a moment, then shook her head slowly. 'No,' she said. 'He was kissing me.'

He nodded as if that was exactly what he had expected. 'Like he was when I saw you,' he guessed, and laughed shortly. 'His timing wasn't very good last night, was it?'

'Oh, Rod, please don't make a big issue out of it!'

She felt suddenly very small and vulnerable. She had always thought the Blairs the most important family in her life until now. Now suddenly these strong-willed, implacable McAdams were taking her over and she felt as if she wanted to run somewhere and hide from them.

Rod, showing all the affronted indignation of a wronged lover; Rose treating her like some kind of low life with designs on Quin, and Quin himself taking up battle on her behalf with his ex-sister-in-law after he had, yet again, put her in jeopardy from the woman's jealousy. The worst part of it all was that she could not even rely on her grandfather to see her point of view, for he was firmly and surely on Quin's side.

'I'm not making a big issue out of it,' Rod denied. 'I just don't like Quin poaching on my territory, that's all. He's never done it before and I wish he'd stick to his own sort.'

'You have no right to talk about me like that,' Laurie protested. 'I'm not something you own, Rod, and I can't be stolen or poached, whatever you call it, because I'm a free agent. And you have no right, either of you, to treat me as if I came with the property. The idea of—of *droit du seigneur* went out long ago, you know.'

'Laurie darling!' He looked quite astounded at her

reaction, and reached for her other hand. 'I'm sorry, I didn't realise you felt so strongly about it.' He leaned across and kissed her cheek lightly, his eyes watching for another indignant reaction. 'Forgive me?'

For a moment Laurie said nothing. Not only were the McAdams strong-minded, they were far too attractive and persuasive too, especially Rod in this mood. He seemed to have completely recovered his good humour and was bent on making up to her. But Laurie was not at all sure that she wanted to go back to what had lately been normal. Certainly Rod was very attractive and she liked him a great deal, but she did not like the idea of belonging to anybody—she had a mind of her own and she would make it up for herself.

'I forgive you, Rod,' she told him. 'As long as you don't get the idea that you have some sort of claim on me.'

'Quin then?' he suggested soft-voiced, and she hastily turned her head away.

'Not Quin either,' she denied. 'I'm a free agent, Rod, with no ties anywhere.'

'All right,' Rod said, turning her head round to him again and kissing her full on her mouth for quite some time. 'I'll remember, if you do,' he told her.

Laurie finished typing the page she was doing and pulled it out of the machine, smiling across at Russ when he looked up. 'You've done that in double-quick time,' he told her. 'Your speed *has* improved, Laurie.'

'I think it has a bit,' she admitted, gratified that the improvement had been noticed.

'In fact,' Russ informed her, 'you've turned out to

be a very efficient secretary.'

'Thank you.' She bobbed her head in a mock bow and smiled.

'I'm glad I listened to Quin and saw you first,' he told her. 'Before I sent to Crathmean for someone from the bureau.'

She looked a little startled until she remembered that it had been Quin who had suggested his brother see her in the first place. 'I'm glad you did too,' she told him.

Russ leaned back in his chair, running one hand through his hair, a gesture he often used and one which was common to all three brothers. There was something on his mind, Laurie thought, and wondered what was behind the somewhat speculative look in his eyes as he studied her for a moment before he spoke again.

'You quite enjoy working for us now that you've got used to us, don't you?' he asked.

Laurie nodded. 'Oh yes, I do. At least,' she qualified, 'I enjoy working for *you*.'

He shook his head slowly as he looked down at his clasped hands. 'Why especially me?' he asked. 'We're all partners and you take dictation from all of us at various times.'

Laurie smiled ruefully as she sought to explain her preference. 'That's true,' she allowed. 'But with Rod I have to wait while he thinks up the right words to suit his mood, and with Quin I can't always keep up and he gets impatient and clucks at me.'

He seemed to find that amusing and laughed, and she wondered why it had never occurred to her before that Russ was just as attractive as either of his brothers.

Rose McAdam, she thought, must be very short-sighted not to have seen that in Russ she had far more than most women expect in a husband.

'Quin wants everything done at supersonic speeds,' he told her. 'But he does give you time to catch up, doesn't he?'

'Only because he hasn't any option unless he wants to write his own letters,' Laurie retorted, and smiled at him. 'Anyway,' she said, 'strictly speaking I actually *work* for you, and I like it that way.'

'You wouldn't be prepared to—to change partners?' he suggested, and smiled wryly at his choice of phrase, while Laurie looked at him curiously for a moment.

'Is there any reason why I should change partners?' she asked at last, and he again looked down at his hands.

'For a while there is,' he told her quietly. 'You see, I have to go away for several weeks, Laurie.'

'Oh! Oh, I see.'

'It isn't permanent,' he went on. 'But there's a new treatment been developed and it could mean that there's a chance I'll walk again, after a fashion. I think it's worth trying.'

'Oh, but that's marvellous!' Laurie said, her eyes shining with genuine pleasure. 'I'm so glad, Russ, I really am.'

'It's all a bit of a gamble, actually,' he confessed. 'But it *might* work, and I'm ready to take the chance.'

'Oh, I'm sure it will!'

'I'll be gone about eight or nine weeks,' he said. 'Starting next week.'

'And naturally you won't be needing me,' she said

178

smiling. 'Well, that's all right, Russ, I understand.'

He looked at her briefly and curiously. 'I wondered if you'd stay on with Quin,' he said.

Laurie stared at him for a moment. 'With Quin?'

He nodded. 'Quin will be taking over my part of the business as well while I'm gone, and he'll need a secretary too. That's what I meant by changing partners.'

'I see.'

He looked at her, anxiously she thought. 'You don't *mind* working for Quin, do you?' he asked, and Laurie sighed.

'I'm not sure,' she told him truthfully. 'I'd love to go on working here, of course, but for Quin——'

'He wants you to, Laurie. In fact'—he laughed shortly—'he expects you to.'

She looked across at him, not doubting for a moment that he was right about that. Quin *would* expect her to go with the job. Laying claim to her as if she was part of the property, she thought, and remembered how she had objected to Rod about the same thing.

'He thinks I go with the furniture, is that it?' she asked, and he frowned.

'No, of course not, my dear,' he assured her. 'But Quin rather thought you'd rather stay on here. I did too.'

'I suppose I would,' she confessed.

'There'll be plenty to do,' he warned her. 'We're expanding all the time and as we said just now, Quin doesn't believe in marking time.'

Laurie remembered something else then, and her heart turned cold as she guessed at the expansion he had mentioned. 'I suppose he'll be turning Clach Aros into a stately home, won't he?' she asked. 'I'd forgotten that.'

For a moment he looked as if he did not understand her, then he smiled and shook his head. 'Indeed he won't,' he said. 'That idea was abandoned before it was ever seriously considered.' The kindly grey eyes looked at her for a moment or two in silence. 'You really hated the idea of that, didn't you, Laurie?'

'I can't think of anything I'd hate more,' she agreed, and he shook his head slowly.

'That's what Quin said,' he told her softly. 'He's the last person to want it turned into a tourist trap, Laurie. He fought it tooth and nail.'

Laurie stared at him for a moment, lips parted, eyes wide with disbelief. Her heart felt as if it had stopped completely and then suddenly it was pounding away at her ribs like a wild thing, and she found her voice at last.

'Quin?' she said huskily. 'Quin fought against it?'

Russ nodded, his eyes faintly quizzical. 'Does that surprise you?' he asked.

'But—but I thought he was the one who——'

He smiled wryly and shook his head at her. 'I know what you thought,' he said. 'Quin told me.'

'Then why didn't he tell *me*?' Laurie protested. 'He let me go on blaming him, and all the time——'

'It wasn't his idea at all,' he assured her.

Laurie looked at him steadily, knowing at the back of her mind what the answer must be, but unwilling yet to face it. 'Then if it wasn't Quin——'

'And it certainly wasn't me,' Russ said quietly, and

she guessed from the expression in his eyes that he knew exactly how she felt.

'It must have been Rod,' she said in a flat voice, and wondered bitterly if she had ever quite so succesfully been made such a fool of before.

'He should have been more honest with you,' Russ said gently.

'So should Quin,' Laurie said, close to tears. 'If only he'd denied it was him, I'd have known it *had* to be Rod.'

He shook his head slowly over his brother's deception. 'Rod was afraid of you thinking badly of him,' he told her, and smiled ruefully. 'He didn't realise until it was too late, you see, how important it was to you, and he didn't want to spoil his image. By then, of course, you had already earmarked Quin as the villain.'

'And what was Quin's reason for letting me go on thinking so?' she asked bitterly. 'Just the reverse, presumably.'

Russ shrugged his shoulders, a little wearily. 'I don't pretend to understand Quin,' he told her. 'I expect he had his own reasons.'

'No doubt!'

'But please don't judge either of them too harshly, Laurie,' he begged gently. 'We're a stubborn breed and I suppose we always run whichever way suits us best.'

'Not you,' Laurie denied quietly. She got up from her desk and walked over to his with the letter she had been typing. 'I know I can trust you, Russ.'

He took the letter from her and laid it down carefully on the desk in front of him. 'Then will you stay here and work for Quin while I'm gone?' he asked softly at last, and Laurie looked at him uneasily.

'Do—do you want me to?'

He looked up and smiled. 'I'd like you to.'

She nodded her head briefly and saw Russ smile as if it pleased him. 'I'll stay,' she told him. 'But we'll probably fight all the time, Russ. You know what it's like, and with you not here to referee——'

He laughed. 'You don't need a referee,' he told her. 'You can cope perfectly well, Laurie.'

'With Quin?' she said doubtfully, already having second thoughts. 'I don't know that I can. I've managed while you've been here to keep the peace but left to his own devices, and obliged to do his own office work and yours as well, I can't see myself lasting very long in those circumstances.'

'But you will try?'

Laurie sighed, then nodded her head. 'I'll try,' she promised.

It had been a rather upsetting day, Laurie thought, and she was glad of a walk after dinner to try and think things out. It was wonderful news that Russ might be able to walk again, of course, but she still had qualms about working for Quin in the same way she had for his brother.

As for the abortive attempt to make Clach Aros into a public show, it hurt her pride badly to realise that Rod had so easily fooled her about that, and she would not easily forgive him. It was, in fact, with the intention of avoiding Rod that she had decided on a walk instead of riding, as she more usually did.

Also by coming this way, through the trees that

bordered the drive, there was less likelihood of her meeting him. She enjoyed walking in the cool shade of the trees, especially after a hot summer's day, and she lifted her face to the almost chill breeze that wafted a smell of rich loam and leaf mould to her.

It was not going to be easy seeing Quin in any role but the one she had originally allocated to him, and she half wished Russ had not told her about his fighting to keep Clach Aros as it was. Bringing Quin over to her side was not only discomfiting but also disturbing to her peace of mind.

It was with a racing heart therefore that she heard him call to her a few minutes later as she walked through to the clearing on the far side of the trees, and instead of turning round, she merely stopped in her tracks one arm round the trunk of a tree, kicking at a pile of earth with the toe of one shoe.

'Your grandpa said I'd find you here,' he told her when he came alongside, and she glanced up and frowned. Her grandfather could be relied upon to tell Quin where she was, whether he thought Laurie wanted to see him or not.

'Were you looking for me?' she asked, still kicking at the soft earth with her toe.

'Not exactly,' he told her, and she guessed he was smiling by the sound of his voice. 'Are you in one of your spoofy moods?' he added. 'You sound as if you've been having words with somebody.'

'No. No, I haven't.' She made no effort to walk on further, but still embraced the tree while he walked round and leaned an elbow on the other side of it, facing her and much too close for her comfort. 'Russ—

Russ told me about his going away,' she said.

'I see.' A brief upward glance revealed a rather surprising warmth in the ice-grey eyes as they looked down at her steadily. 'I expect he also mentioned that I wanted you to carry on in the same job with me, did he?' She nodded. 'And that's the reason for your looking as solemn as a little owl?'

'I didn't know I was,' she said defensively.

He lifted her chin with one hand and smiled down at her. 'You look as if you have serious doubts about it all,' he told her. 'And I can't think why you should.'

'Can't you?' She looked up at him, holding his gaze for longer than she meant to, but it was so hard to look away again. 'I warned Russ we should probably come to blows, but he seems to think it'll be O.K.'

'Of course it will,' he assured her blithely. 'Is that all that's giving you the glooms?'

He must know, Laurie thought. Her grandfather would have told him that she was upset about Rod's deception, and she put up a hand to release his hold on her chin. 'It's all I want to talk about,' she told him. 'Except——' She hesitated, wondering suddenly how she was going to word her apology. 'I have to say I'm sorry.'

'To me?' She nodded. 'What for?'

She looked up at him reproachfully. 'Oh, you know what for,' she told him. 'I'm sure Grandpa must have told you. I—I've just learned that Rod was the one who wanted to exhibit Clach Aros, not you.'

'That's right.'

She pouted, but hastily lowered her gaze when she saw that strange, intense look in his eyes again. 'You could have told me I was wrong,' she told him.

'And spoiled your illusions?' He laughed softly. 'Poor little Laurie, now you have to face the fact that even the most romantic of us has a strong commercial streak!'

For a long time she said nothing, although her brain was spinning round and round with all sorts of unanswerable questions, and he seemed content to just lean against the tree and watch her face. 'I—I seem to have had a lot of wrong ideas about you,' she said at last, and wondered that the admission came so easily. 'I'm sorry, Quin.'

For a moment he neither said nor did anything, then he leaned over and kissed her very gently on her mouth. 'You're forgiven,' he said softly. 'Now smile, will you? I hate to see you looking so gloomy.'

'I'm not really gloomy,' she denied. 'I—I just had a lot to think about, and I didn't think I could face Rod without being absolutely bitchy to him, so I came out here to avoid him.'

He was laughing, but she did not even feel angry about it. '*Can* you be bitchy?' he asked, and she could not resist the wry smile that tilted her mouth.

'You should know,' she told him.

'I *should* know,' he echoed. 'You had your knife into me from the word go, didn't you? Now don't deny it,' he added hastily when she would have argued. 'I know why, and to a certain extent I understand your feelings, but sometimes you were such a pugnacious little devil I could have cheerfully spanked you!'

He was speaking, she noticed, in the past tense and she laughed suddenly, as if a weight had been lifted

185

off her mind. 'You'd have been sorry if you had,' she told him. 'I can bite very hard. And you couldn't really blame me for getting mad with you when you always treat me like a little girl. It's infuriating for a grown woman to have to put up with such indignity.'

He grinned at her, his face close to hers and that oddly disturbing look in his eyes again as he looked at her mouth. 'A grown woman,' he echoed softly. 'Yes, I suppose you are.'

'Of course I am!'

'Then I'd better start treating you like one.'

'You had,' she agreed firmly.

He reached across the few feet that separated them and pulled her towards him until she was pressed so close she had to lean back her head to look up at him. Her pulses were leaping wildly and she felt oddly breathless as he looked at her steadily for a long moment before he bent his head.

His mouth was at once fiercely possessive and gentle and she made no protest at all as she closed her eyes, her arms sliding up round his neck until her fingers held handfuls of the thick fair hair that grew in his neck.

'Quin!'

He laughed softly against her ear, his voice muffled in the thickness of her hair. 'Is that grown up enough for you?'

She put her hands on his chest and pushed him away from her, her eyes wide and a little wary, anxious too as she looked up at him. 'I'm not sure I——'

Before she could go on he brushed her lips with his own and smiled. 'I love you,' he told her softly. 'Does that make it all right, my sweet love?'

He had called her that once before, Laurie remembered vaguely, and nodded her head. 'I expect so,' she said huskily, and lifted her face to him again.

'Now this is going to make things quite different,' he said when he released her again and rested his face on her hair. 'It looks as if I shall have to get another secretary after all.'

Laurie stirred briefly in his arms. 'Why?' she asked.

'Because I don't think you and work would mix very well,' he told her. 'You'd be far too much of a distraction, my love, I always thought you would be.'

'But you were so insistent that I should work for you while Russ was away.'

He laughed softly and kissed her ear. 'Only because I thought it was the only way to have you near me,' he told her, then sighed deeply. 'Now I suppose I shall have to get Miss Grieve's bureau to send me some suitable females to look over.'

Laurie raised her head then, her wide blue eyes darkly shining and with a determined gleam in their depths. 'Well, you tell Miss Grieve,' she told him firmly, 'not to send anyone under forty or in the least bit glamorous.'

Quin laughed again. 'Now I'm going to marry *you*, I shan't even notice what she looks like,' he vowed, and Laurie made a face.

'I hope you mean that.'

His arms tightened round her until she had not even breath to protest. 'When I'm married to you, my love, I shan't have time for anybody else.'

'I seem to remember,' Laurie murmured dreamily, 'that I once said I could no more marry you than fly to the moon.'

'You did?' He looked down at her curiously, that warm, intense look in his eyes again. 'That was a very rash statement to make. Who did you tell that to?'

Laurie smiled, her hands rumpling his hair at the back of his neck, her eyes glowing with laughter. 'Old Margaret McKinnon,' she told him, and he laughed.

'The old matchmaker! Did she have a go at you too?' Laurie nodded. 'You know, strictly speaking all this is her fault,' he went on. '*She* put the idea into my head about marrying you, and here I am about to do just that.'

'Are you?' Laurie asked, kissing his chin. 'I don't remember you asking me yet.'

Quin chuckled deeply and hugged her close again. 'I know you, my sweet love,' he told her. 'You'll never be able to resist the chance to live at Clach Aros again, will you?'

Laurie knew she never would, but she was glad it wasn't the only reason, and when he kissed her again she wondered if it even mattered at all.

OMNIBUS

The 3-in-1 HARLEQUIN — only $1.75 per volume

Here is a great new exciting idea from Harlequin. THREE GREAT ROMANCES — complete and unabridged — BY THE SAME AUTHOR — in one deluxe paperback volume — for the unbelievably low price of only $1.75 per volume.

We have chosen some of the finest works of world-famous authors and reprinted them in the 3-in-1 Omnibus. Almost 600 pages of pure entertainment for just $1.75. A TRULY "JUMBO" READ!

The following pages list some of the exciting novels in this series.

Climb aboard the Harlequin Omnibus now! The coupon below is provided for your convenience in ordering.

HARLEQUIN OMNIBUS

THE 3-IN-1 VOLUME — EACH BY THE SAME
AUTHOR — EACH ONLY $1.75

HARLEQUIN OMNIBUS

☐ CATHERINE AIRLIE

Doctor Overboard (# 979)
Nobody's Child (#1258)
A Wind Sighing (#1328)
$1.75

☐ VIOLET WINSPEAR ②

Bride's Dilemma (#1008)
Tender Is The Tyrant (#1208)
The Dangerous Delight (#1344)
$1.75

☐ KATHRYN BLAIR

Doctor Westland (# 954)
Battle Of Love (#1038)
Flowering Wilderness (#1148)
$1.75

☐ ROSALIND BRETT

The Girl At Whitedrift (#1101)
Winds Of Enchantment (#1176)
Brittle Bondage (#1319)
$1.75

THE 3-IN-1 VOLUME — EACH BY THE SAME
AUTHOR — EACH ONLY $1.75